PAUL SINHA'S
REAL BRITISH
CITIZENSHIP TEST

PAUL SINHA'S

REAL
BRITISH
CITIZENSHIP
TEST

Everything you need to know
to call yourself British

PORTICO

Many thanks to my parents, without whose sense of adventure I would be nothing; to my sister Lily for her support; to all my friends for providing the inspiration; and to Sally Carter, for whose incredible hard work I will be forever in debt.

First published in the United Kingdom in 2015 by
Portico
1 Gower Street
London
WC1E 6HD

An imprint of Pavilion Books Company Ltd

ISBN 978-1-91023-229-3

A CIP catalogue record for this book is available from the British Library.

10 9 8 7 6 5 4 3 2 1

Reproduction by Mission Productions Ltd, Hong Kong
Printed and bound by GPS Group Ltd, Slovenia

This book can be ordered direct from the publisher at www.pavilionbooks.com

SO YOU WANT TO BE BRITISH?

YOU HAVE MADE A FANTASTIC
CHOICE. IT IS GREAT FUN LIVING
ON THIS SUN-STARVED GROUP OF
ISLANDS. BUT BEING BRITISH IS
NOT JUST ABOUT TICKING BOXES.
IT IS A STATE OF MIND. CULTURAL
INTEGRATION IS A KEY PART OF
BECOMING BRITISH, AND TO DO
THAT YOU NEED TO KNOW WHAT
MAKES THE NATION TICK...

Britain is an extremely diverse country. A combination of twentieth-century immigration, and a population now more glued to television and smartphones than ever, has subtly altered what the shared values are. But there are shared values. To try to establish these, in 2005 the Home Office devised a Citizenship Test with an accompanying syllabus that was messy, inconsistent, not always truthful and in many cases already out of date. This short guide is an attempt to redress that, and provide a more modern, relevant look at what you need to know to call yourself British. For a start:

TO BE BRITISH, you do not need to be able to name Henry VIII's wives in order. How can this possibly be true when most of the indigenous population cannot complete said task? You do need to know of his existence, and that his rather misogynistic attitudes towards women would not be tolerated now.

TO BE BRITISH, you do not have to be able to dance around a maypole. But it would help if you knew something about Britain's contribution to contemporary music.

TO BE BRITISH, you do not need to be a functioning alcoholic. But you do need to know that during your time here, many of your most beloved friends and colleagues will be functioning alcoholics. And that they are good people.

TO BE BRITISH, you need to know that looking at France and Germany in an admiring way will eventually get you into bother.

TO BE BRITISH is to understand the quirks of the major cities, and to understand why a booted skinhead in a pub in Brighton may well have a very different agenda to one in Portsmouth.

TO BE BRITISH is to be able to express one's political views loudly and boorishly to anyone who will listen, and maintain utter contempt for modern politicians and the systems that prop them up.

TO BE BRITISH is to live your life with an unrestrained passion for the sport of football and all its inherent beauty, while simultaneously bitterly hating every single football club that isn't the one you support.

TO BE BRITISH is to live in a land of flaws and contradictions, and still feel like the luckiest person on earth.

This is the land of great literature, music, culture and cinema. It brought the world penicillin, television and the theory of evolution. It is also the land of Katie Hopkins. This guide aims to help you through modern minefields, and give you an idea of how to make the most of your time here. I hope you enjoy it.

ABERDEEN

Barring the large-scale immigration of aardvarks into the UK, this guide was always likely to begin with Aberdeen. Nicknamed 'The Granite City', first impressions suggest a dour and monochrome port with a microclimate that Sir Ranulph Fiennes would consider to be a bit parky. Second and third impressions do nothing to change that view.

Nonetheless, Aberdeen has a confidence derived from its oil-based wealth, it is the birthplace of comedian Graeme Garden and football legend Denis Law, and it has won Britain in Bloom an impressive ten times. Incidentally, scientists have calculated that no matter where you are in the UK, you are at least 170 miles from Aberdeen.

TOP TIP

Ingratiate yourself with the locals by being able to recite all the details about the 1983 Cup Winners' Cup Final.

ACCIDENT AND EMERGENCY

A
B
C
D
E
F
G
H
I
J
K
L
M
N
O
P
Q
R
S
T
U
V
W
X
Y
Z

Thanks to greedy politicians mismanaging the National Health Service to line their own pockets, the number of hospitals offering an Accident and Emergency service is sadly dwindling. This, however, is still your first port of call in a medical emergency. Please have a clear idea of what constitutes an emergency. Crushing chest pain, broken bones, worsening asthma, the complete loss of movement down one side of your body – these are very valid reasons to attend A&E. Toothache, misplacing your glasses, hangover, the inability to solve the last few clues in the *Times* crossword – please stay at home. One quick glance at the average A&E department reveals a gruesome vision of hell with some of the most overworked staff in the country. You will have a long wait. Bring a book, or for those of you who aren't readers, have Angry Birds at the ready. And try not to go on a Friday or Saturday night, when the place is overrun by unfortunate souls carrying acute injuries caused by spilling the wrong pint belonging to the wrong bloke in the wrong pub.

TOP TIP

Don't call the nurses 'love' or 'darling' unless you want to queue for a really long time.

ADELE

As one moves into middle age, the ability to understand and appreciate modern music starts to diminish alarmingly, and the struggle to distinguish between Iggy Azalea and Azealia Banks becomes an epic voyage of discovery. So thank the lord for Adele for keeping it simple. A true British superstar, her mellifluous voice adorns songs so competent and satisfactory that her album titles *19* and *21* refer to what the critics rated them out of 30. Much like Mumford & Sons, Adele is comfort music for those of us who don't really have the inclination to find out what a Nicki Minaj is.

PRACTICE QUESTION

What line follows 'Let the sky fall'?

ALTERNATIVE COMEDY

Once upon a time, stand-up comedy was the preserve of overweight middle-aged men provoking near-hysteria with their carefully honed jokes about the evil mother-in-law, the smelly Pakistani neighbours, and the hilarious cultural misunderstandings that ensue when an Englishman, a Scotsman and a particularly dense Irishman walk into a bar. Then came the revolution. At a point zero estimated to be circa 1979, an army of angry young comedians attempted to overthrow the stifling conservatism of the past with radical jokes about Thatcher, the hard-working Pakistani neighbours, and what it was like being a woman. Some people loved it, some people yearned for an imagined halcyon era where you could 'call a spade a spade', but there is no doubt the revolution was successful.

TOP TIP

1. Don't sit at the front, unless you have no self-esteem issues whatsoever.

2. Texting while a comedian is on stage? You are Satan's spawn. Please leave the country.

Because now 'alternative comedians' are everywhere. They are judging talent shows, selling out arenas, answering general knowledge questions and attempting to inspire a revolution by urging people not to vote.

As a result of all this, every town or city has its own comedy club. Go along to watch, it is a useful exercise in assessing the pulse of the nation. Lefty diatribes are out. Mocking the guy in the checked shirt who is clearly homosexual, telling tales of the hilariously racist (and fictional) things their grandparents have said, and dismissing the people of a neighbouring town as inbred are definitely in.

ALTON TOWERS

The former seat of the Earl of Shrewsbury has been, for many decades, Britain's best-loved theme park. The theme is queuing. The rides are impressively terrifying, and if you have kids, do take them there at least once. They will love you for it. Just be prepared to spend most of your day standing in a line wondering just how obnoxious so many of Britain's teenagers are. Nonetheless, it is nice that there is now a valid reason to visit Staffordshire.

TOP TIP

Eat somewhere else. Anywhere else. Just not at Alton Towers.

ANGEL OF THE NORTH

Britain, despite its imperial past, does not really do ostentatious public sculpture, to the extent that there are really only two examples that are well known nationally. The statue mistakenly known as Eros in Piccadilly Circus is a dreary piece of work in a dreary public space largely occupied by dreary tourists, labouring under the entirely risible misconception that Piccadilly Circus is cool.

The Angel of the North, however, is an altogether different beast. It is the most British of statues, overlooking as it does an otherwise dispiriting stretch of the A1 and A167. It is not conventionally beautiful, it is rather unclear what it actually represents, and yet somehow it works. Britain in a nutshell.

PRACTICE QUESTION

How tall is the Angel of the North? Whatever you guess, double it.

THE APPRENTICE

This television show is one of the most popular ever broadcast by the BBC. This seems inexplicable until you realise just how much the British enjoy making themselves feel better by watching irredeemable morons going about their business.

The premise of the show is simple. A terrible human being repeatedly tells a group of terrible human beings that they are, indeed, terrible human beings. Each week a contestant is fired, and thankfully they are never heard of again.

The winner, chosen in a random and arbitrary way that is impossible to comprehend, is offered a partnership with Lord Sugar. It is hard to imagine a less appealing prize unless you watch old episodes of *Bullseye* on YouTube (highly recommended). In the opinion of the author, the lack of self-awareness of this relentless parade of narcissistic dullards makes for wearying television. I am prepared to admit, it is wearying *successful* television, and it is important to know just what it is that your work colleagues are gossiping about at the water-cooler.

PRACTICE QUESTION

Explain the difference between 'self-confident' and 'arrogant bellend'.

ARGOS

This guide is hopefully full of useful tips. None of them are quite as essential as this one. If you are thinking of buying anything – Argos probably sells it cheaper. Let the middle classes fritter their money away in more expensive stores of greater repute. Do not be put off by Argos's ugly designs, be brave and walk in. Be patient with their bizarre purchasing system, and suddenly you will find that the world is your oyster. Argos is a temple to pragmatic, good-value consumerism and provides everything you could ever require in an emergency.

TOP TIP

For God's sake keep the receipt.

TOP TIPS

WEDDINGS

A nice wedding is one of the most civilising social affairs British life can offer you. It is a great opportunity to celebrate the fact that you and your best mate won't be seeing each other much any more, and it is important to get the etiquette right.

1 If it is a religious ceremony, bring a book. Preferably quite a long one.

2 Black tie means dinner jacket. Anything else means suit and tie. You may think you are being a loveable maverick by not adhering to these rules. The bride and groom will hold their grudge for a very long time.

3 'If any person here present knows of any just or lawful impediment why these two persons may not be joined in marriage….' Do not even think about it.

4 The wedding list is there for a reason. It is the stuff they really need. Don't buy them a framed Garfield cartoon just to be different.

5 This is the bride's day. What you might consider to be 'cheeky banter' could ruin her life.

6 The wine at the table is to be shared equally among those seated there, no matter what ideas you may have to the contrary.

7 Laugh at the best man's speech. He is dying out there.

8 There is a time and a place for overdoing it on the champagne. This is definitely neither the time nor the place for slumping in a chair and weeping inconsolably, while shouting out, 'It is never going to be my day, is it?'

DAVID ATTENBOROUGH

There is one simple reason why David Attenborough is in this guide. That is because there is a decent case to be made that he is Britain's greatest living person. Somehow he has managed to go through life metaphorically touching things and watching them turn to gold.

One might argue that the real geniuses behind his amazing nature documentaries are the production team. But I don't know their names. I know his name. And like the rest of the nation I both know and love his voice, as he gently explains the worlds of chimpanzee mating calls, wildebeest migration and the feeding patterns of the tuatara.

Nowadays, so much television is rooted in the concept of the lowest common denominator. Never pass up the chance to celebrate a man whose remarkable body of work remains a high-water mark in broadcasting history.

TOP TIP

Buy the box sets. It may keep your kids quiet for hours.

JANE AUSTEN

'It is a truth universally acknowledged, that a single man in possession of a good fortune must be in want of a wife.' And so it came to pass that *Pride and Prejudice*, one of the most famous novels of all time, began with stuffy, patriarchal nonsense that seemed to misunderstand the words 'truth', 'universally acknowledged' and 'must'.

And this is the highlight of Austen's celebrated oeuvre, a series of novels that document social and romantic dilemmas that can most politely be described as 'first world problems'. Characters who run the demographical gamut from middle-class to upper-middle-class flirt, swoon, have temporary mishaps and eventually marry. It is truly thrilling stuff, and the novels have become so firmly established as an archetype of what it means to be English that there is even documented evidence of some men having read one or two of the books.

But the main reason you need to be au fait with Austen is that from 2017 she will be replacing Charles Darwin on the £10 note. Know your banknotes. To understand a nation's culture it is good to know just which historical figures are revered. Jane Austen may seem like a bland choice, but in a hundred years when Kerry Katona is on the £10 note, now will seem like a glorious time to be alive.

TOP TIP

Read the 2009 novel *Pride and Prejudice and Zombies*, which updates the original novel while making only minor alterations to the plot.

BATH

If you have somehow found yourself living or working in Bath, then congratulations are in order as you have done very well in life. It is a city that walks the tightrope between heart-warmingly pretty and irritatingly twee and always seems to come out on top, no matter how expensive that scone and cup of tea are. Like a lot of towns and cities, the atmosphere of genteel civility is rather rudely interrupted at the weekend, when the city plays host to scores of stag and hen nights that seem to have no interest in Roman baths, and even less in the Jane Austen Centre. Do not make eye contact with them.

TOP TIP

If your only clean jumper is a rugby top, you are in luck. This is one city where a rugby top is seen as the very height of fashion.

THE BEATLES

More than 50 years ago, two talented songwriters met a talented guitarist and brought in a guy who could play the drums a bit. The result is the stuff of music legend, as every Liverpudlian will tell you within ten minutes of meeting them. They started by reducing female fans to hysteria. They went on to reduce music critics to admiring nods of approval thanks to an almost uniquely varied musical career that saw them morph from clean-cut pop stars to the acceptable face of illicit drug use. It doesn't matter if you find lyrics about silver hammers ludicrous, it doesn't matter if you don't believe them when they suggest that all they really want is to hold your hand. The fact remains that to be British is to understand why The Beatles are revered across the globe in a manner that no number of missed notes from Sir Paul McCartney will ever tarnish.

TOP TIP

Don't ask about Yoko.

DAVID BECKHAM

What you must understand is this. David Beckham is better than you. Every time he smiles, thousands of fashion photographers start counting the dollars. He is married to a pop star of sorts. His kids all dress far better than you. He once scored from the halfway line, in fact his footballing career is littered with superlative goals (and disappointing contributions in major national tournaments). He is living proof that it is possible to emerge from humble beginnings in Leytonstone to become a likeable, walking, talking combination of clothes horse, ambassador and moneymaking machine. You can beat him at Trivial Pursuit. But in almost everything else he is better than you.

TOP TIP

Play him at
Trivial Pursuit.

BELFAST

Belfast does get a bad press. For decades it has suffered levels of sectarian hatred that are difficult to understand unless your degree course was in 'Battle of the Boyne'.

But underneath the surface of age-old prejudices is a bright, hard-drinking city clamouring to be heard. One of its two airports is named after George Best. What other city would name its airport after an alcoholic serial adulterer? New York.

TOP TIP

1. Don't dress as a soldier for a fancy dress party.

2. Never ask 'Is it called Derry or Londonderry?'

A B C D E F G H I J K L M N O P Q R S T U V W X Y Z

BIG BROTHER

In 2000, Channel 4 started a bold televisual project to place a bunch of strangers in a house together and watch how their social relationships developed. It was an ambitious anthropological experiment, and the duplicity of 'Nasty Nick' gripped the nation. Unfortunately something terrible happened to many of the contestants in Big Brother 1. They became famous.

As a result, every subsequent series featured the same cacophonous combination of sad, attention-seeking wannabes, desperate to make their name by being as appalling as possible. What started as anthropology soon turned into a prolonged audition for the gossip pages of very bad magazines.

Sociopathy, racism and fiery tempers all became valid career moves. And the celebrity version of the show proved no better, as a selection of has-beens sold their souls to pay their tax bills.

Luckily, both versions of the show are now consigned to the television dustbin. Or to give it its proper title, Channel 5. Take an opportunity to watch ten minutes or so of the show and console yourself with the following thought: you are much better than any of these people.

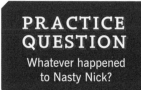

PRACTICE QUESTION

Whatever happened to Nasty Nick?

BINGE DRINKING

So here is the deal. Britain prides itself on its levels of alcoholic intoxication. Every weekend, boys and girls prowl the streets looking for bars and clubs to try to get laid, or at least for those who are not single, have an evening that they will remember fondly in years to come. The problem is that nobody is terrified of getting too drunk. They are terrified of not getting drunk at all.

```
TOP TIP
You don't have to say yes
to every round.
```

Thus from about 9pm onwards, casualties start piling up. Mark has punched his mate Gary for saying that Wayne Rooney is overrated. Sarah can't stop crying because nobody has complimented her on her new dress. Tel didn't realise that a tandoori mixed grill takes some time to cook, and is now racially abusing the staff. Shelley's heels simply aren't practical and she has fractured her ankle. Jason has stolen a car and crashed it into a tree, killing himself and a fox. LEGEND.

And every weekend the same cycle of destruction plays out. It is understandable that people who have worked hard all week want to let off some steam, but nobody seems to be slightly bothered about pacing themselves.

BIRMINGHAM

In January 2015, a so-called 'terrorism expert' on Fox News claimed that Birmingham was totally Muslim. In the ensuing uproar he apologised and called it a 'beautiful city'.

It is hard to know which statement was more nonsensical, but contrary to popular belief, Birmingham does have beautiful bits. It also famously claims to have 'more canals than Venice'. The truth of this is up for debate, but it does have more Brummies, cricket stadia, conference hotels and ring roads than Venice.

It is the home of the revolutionary Balti restaurant – which is like other Indian restaurants, only the food is cooked in a dish called a Balti. It has a functional Chinatown complete with astonishing portion sizes, and a gay village. Both sit within staggering distance of each other. What is not to love?

Most importantly, it is Britain's second city. So ignore the haters and get to know it.

TOP TIP

I once walked into a restaurant in Birmingham's Chinatown and said, 'Table for two please.' The guy replied, 'I don't work here.' Don't do that.

JAMES BOND

Only in Britain can a reckless philanderer and cold-blooded murderer be the ultimate male icon for the nation. I have yet to meet anyone who has actually read any of Ian Fleming's books. They may be excellent for all I know. But Bond's fame springs from the enduring series of glossy films in which his physical prowess, insouciant wit and remarkable track record with women has become a template for what every red-blooded heterosexual British man would like to achieve. The idea that James Bond is a very *British* hero seems strangely ironic given that many British men have barely mastered text messaging, let alone sophisticated gadgetry. In addition, James Bond's unwillingness to order a pint of lager would have him labelled as 'probably gay' by most of his fan base.

Nonetheless, he is undoubtedly as British as it gets. It is every heterosexual man's job to watch the films and strive to his levels of perfection. Good luck with that.

PRACTICE QUESTION

Count up just how many people James Bond has killed over the years, and then wonder why it might be that many nations seem to have an issue with Britain.

BREAKFAST

Britain does not have a healthy diet, and nowhere can this be seen more clearly than at breakfast time. Whereas other nations seem to see breakfast as an opportunity to combine the vitamins and carbohydrates required to wake up the human body, the British take their inspiration from the cookbook '1001 Ways to Cook a Pig'.

Bacon, sausages, black pudding. The butcher has gone to great lengths to exploit as many areas of the pig as possible, including its congealed blood. The result is a meal that is far more tasty than croissants could ever dream of being, but also a major step on the road to cardiovascular catastrophe. It is a testament to the sheer deliciousness of the pig that nobody cares.

TOP TIP

Breakfast buffets. Just because you *can* 'eat as much as you like' does not mean that you should.

BRITAIN'S GOT TALENT

This is an annual competition to establish the most popular variety act in Britain or Hungary. Hosted by man-children icons Ant and Dec, its chief claim to fame is having launched the career of Susan Boyle, who stunned the world with the extraordinary revelation that it is possible to be both plain, and a fully functioning human being with talent.

It is a show that accurately reflects the tastes of a nation. When dance troupe Diversity won, it was seen as a triumph for the concept of a multicultural society. Now it is seen mainly as an annual celebration of unusually talented pets.

TOP TIP

Teach your dog to dance. Inevitable riches await.

LONDON

It is the capital of the United Kingdom! It is one of the most ethnically diverse places on earth! A four-bedroom house in Bury costs as much as afternoon tea at Claridge's! The traffic never moves, the people are unfriendly, and the city is only ever one wrongful shooting away from a full-scale riot.

I am a Londoner. I both love it with a passion and totally understand its limitations. I don't judge you if you have no intentions ever to visit or live here, but if you are planning to, here are some things you will need to know.

1 When the Oyster card was first introduced, it seemed exotic and unnecessarily intrusive. The truth is that it is very user-friendly. If you see an empty station, top up your card and avoid the later scenario of being completely stuck behind dozens of Japanese tourists.

2 Wherever it is you would like to travel to, black cabs are only the answer if you are a multimillionaire.

3 If you have not bought property already, forget it. The property prices in London offer value in the same way that billiards offers excitement. Don't even look in an estate agent's window if you have a heart condition.

4 Londoners have a reputation for being rude, which is frankly unfair. However, if you stand on the wrong side of an escalator, you will soon regret it.

5 If you buy a pint in a central London pub, don't assume that your fiver will cover it.

6 If you like your food, make use of the ethnic diversity of London. There are several Indian areas including Southall, Tooting and Whitechapel. For Caribbean try Brixton, for Korean head to New Malden, and for Vietnamese go to Hoxton. For French, your best bet is the Eurostar to Paris.

7 Expense is becoming a regular theme. Don't visit London unless you have a friend to stay with, or you are happy to spend £200 on an Ibis hotel.

8 If you are thinking of visiting London on a Sunday, avoid all thoughts of using public transport. It is such a shell of a service that it can take up to an hour to get from Tooting Bec to Tooting Broadway.

9 A lot of food outlets evoke the magic of Kentucky Fried Chicken by replacing 'Kentucky' with another US state name. It doesn't matter if it is Tennessee, Illinois or Arkansas Fried Chicken, they all serve instantly regrettable food.

10 If a mugger tells you they have a knife, they are almost certainly telling you the truth.

London is not an easy city. It is overcrowded, expensive and busy. Public transport is cramped and unwieldy, teenagers are prone to violence, and you will never, ever be able to afford your dream home. But it is a city of history and culture, of large parks and elegant bridges, of underrated neighbourhoods and outstanding restaurants. It is not for everyone. But for a lot of people it is the greatest show on earth. And remember that so much of London – the walk around St James's Park, the view across the Thames to St Paul's, seeing artistic treasures at the National Gallery – is absolutely free.

BRITISH MUSEUM

Only fifty per cent of this title is true. It is certainly a museum, one of the biggest in the world, and a two-hour visit is pitifully short of what is required to do it justice. It is only British in the sense that the vast majority of people who pillaged and plundered the world to bring the exhibits here were British.

One might expect to see typically 'British' exhibits like Magna Carta, royal regalia or historic maps. Instead, we get Greek friezes, Egyptian mummies and Asian drinking vessels. It is an impressive, if exhausting, tribute to the light fingers of archaeologists past.

TOP TIP
Unless you have a genuine passion for archaeology, I would give this one a miss.

BUDGET AIRLINES

Very few natives will care to admit it, but one of the greatest things about being British is that the rest of Europe is on your doorstep. It used to be that a short break to one of Europe's great cities was an expensive indulgence fit only for the most upwardly mobile. That was before easyJet and Ryanair revolutionised the travel industry. Massive fare reductions were accompanied by a reduction in services offered. Out went comfort, in-flight meals and leg space.

TOP TIP

Seriously. Give yourself plenty of time to get to the departure gate.

In came scratchcards and a half-hour walk from Duty Free to the departure gate. Ryanair's signature – using European airports that are a three-hour bus ride away from the advertised destination – has done nothing to dent its popularity. People like value for money.

It represents great news for the British, and for the takings of sex clubs in Prague and Budapest. It is less good news for the Catalan ambience of La Rambla, a once mighty pedestrian thoroughfare now submerged every weekend by the sound of squealing drunks.

ROBERT BURNS

Scotland, of course, has much to recommend it. But perhaps nothing illustrates the concept of cultural divide more than attitudes towards their national poet, Robert Burns. To any sane mind, his words are as far from dulcet as it is possible to imagine, a cacophony of mismatched syllables struggling to come together to create anything resembling phonetic harmony. Where other great poets were inspired by nature, love, religion and myth, Robert Burns addressed dirges to a haggis, a mouse, and a toothache.

The author, however, grudgingly accepts that celebrating your national poet is culturally admirable, and Burns Night is an excuse to get drunk and is therefore, by definition, *a good thing*.

TOP TIP

If you have an English accent, never ever attempt to read the poetry of Robert Burns out loud.

CARDIFF

Cardiff is the capital, largest city, cultural hub and spiritual centre of a plucky subdivision of Britain called Wales. It is one of 517 British towns and cities for which the term 'hard drinking' barely does it justice. It has a castle. The castle has peacocks walking among its grounds. Rarely will one see birds less happy with their lot in life. Apart from on the ITV show *Loose Women*.

It lies on the wonderfully named River Taff, but even better than that it has a neighbourhood called Splott, which is every bit as picturesque as the name suggests. Lottery money has been kind to Cardiff, with urban regeneration as far as the eye can see. It is a great city, as appealing for fans of *Doctor Who* (see page 56), as it is to aficionados of Rugby Union.

It also contains Caroline Street, nicknamed 'Chippy Alley' due to its density of fast food outlets. It is worth knowing that in 2010 South Wales police described the street as 'a honey pot for antisocial behaviour'. This is police speak for 'Run. Run for your lives. You are about to get punched'.

TOP TIP

Get through any conversation with the locals by saying 'Leigh Halfpenny is such a legend', repeatedly and as if you mean it.

CHARIOTS OF FIRE

One of a selection of movies that represent a core syllabus of British culture, this Oscar-winning film evokes a bygone era, one so different from today that it was perfectly possible for a white man to win Olympic gold in the men's 100 metres. An era of class prejudice, subtle anti-Semitism and sports stars of modest means and ambition who simply wanted to do their best for God and country – and who would never dream of having an emotional breakdown if they fell short.

The scene on the cross-channel voyage, where Olympic hopeful Harold Abrahams is sat at the piano belting out the songs of Gilbert and Sullivan, illustrates a simple maxim: 'things have changed'.

TOP TIP

Bring hankies.

CHINA

Famously, there are over one billion people living in China. At the last count, the number of Chinese people living in the UK is not that far off. Thanks to Britain's maritime tradition, Chinese people have been making their home in this country for generations. The first Chinatown in Western Europe was actually set up in Liverpool. Manchester, Newcastle, Birmingham and, of course, London have followed suit. This is very good news for lovers of fine food.

Chinese restaurants and takeaways are now something of a phenomenon and can be found in pretty much all towns and cities across the land. Customer service does not appear to be that high a priority, but rather like with English breakfasts, disembowelling the pig yields spectacular results. In fact, the only thing the Chinese seem to love more than great food is a massive bet, which certainly puts a smile on the faces of bookmakers up and down the country. Someone needs to tell the Chinese that nobody has yet developed a successful system for roulette.

TOP TIP

Many 'specialist' restaurants offer more exotic fare such as pig's ears, cold jellyfish and duck's tongue. Do not be tempted. These dishes were not really designed for Western palates.

CHURCH

For a nation that is not well versed in the scriptures, and which often sees religious leaders as figures of fun, Britain can be very protective about its own religious heritage. Yes, we are mostly atheists and agnostics, and Sunday attendances have been dwindling for many decades now, but nonetheless, the House of Lords has no shortage of religious representatives, and even in its most conservative and repressive moments, Christianity is seen by most as a far more attractive prospect than sharia.

Most importantly of all, a church is a terribly scenic place to have a wedding. It is quite commonplace for families looking for wedding venues to suddenly rediscover their religious beliefs. In addition to that, singing is, and always has been, fun.

TOP TIP

'And did those feet in ancient time…' Belt it out. It is a *great* tune.

WINSTON CHURCHILL

Never in the field of British history can one man have been admired by so many. Churchill *is* the daddy. Voted 'Greatest Briton' in a BBC poll, the interesting thing about Winston Churchill is that he was by no means universally liked. Especially not by my Grandad.

Gruff, temperamental and often contemptuous to the point of bigoted, he was nonetheless a man of obscene talents – skilled painter and Nobel Prize-winning author to name but two. He was also funny in a way that most of us could barely dream of. But most importantly of all, in Britain's darkest hour he had the charisma and leadership qualities to convince a nation that blood, sweat, toil and tears were definitely the way forward. If it wasn't for him, we might all be making a very ham-fisted attempt to speak German.

TOP TIP

To be fair, it is important to take some of the poll results with a massive dollop of salt. Edward Jenner, whose smallpox vaccine saved the lives of millions, finished behind Robbie Williams.

CORONATION STREET

A
B
C
D
E
F
G
H
I
J
K
L
M
N
O
P
Q
R
S
T
U
V
W
X
Y
Z

Can it really be 55 years? For more than half a century the lives of working-class Weatherfielders have been beamed into living rooms across the land, and it is now the longest-running television soap opera the world has ever seen. Initially rooted in the minutiae of the mundane, where an under-seasoned hotpot might have been seen as a dramatic plot development, the show's scope has expanded to such an extent that fatal accidents are to be expected, murder is greeted with little more than a raised eyebrow, and marital fidelity is seen as a laughably naïve fantasy.

TOP TIP

Best not to get too emotionally attached to the characters. They will be dead/disfigured/on a one-way trip to visit a sickly relative before you know it.

The show's success is so absolute that in 1985 the BBC created their London equivalent, *EastEnders* (see page 60), with less convincing accents and an even higher body count.

CRICKET

In this guide, great care has been taken to use the words 'Britain' or 'United Kingdom' rather than 'England'. No such caution is required on the subject of cricket. There have been some fine Welsh, Scottish and Irish cricketers over the years, but true cricket obsession seems like a peculiarly English thing.

To many, cricket is an insufferably pompous affair with Byzantine rules and etiquette, and less of a sport and more an arcane relic of Empire, with its accompanying sense of cultural superiority. To others, that is exactly what makes cricket great. Many people hate cricket because it is nothing like football. To others, that is exactly what makes cricket great.

But apart from its inherent style and aesthetic beauty, what makes cricket great is the number of unsung heroes who live out the weekends of their middle-aged years batting, bowling and occasionally fielding in village and club matches up and down the land. The genteel atmosphere, the spirit of teamwork, cooperation and religious tolerance, and the sublime, freshly made egg mayonnaise sandwiches all contribute to a tableau of Britain that invigorates the soul.

That said, it is rare to meet someone who had a cricket-deprived childhood, but who then grew to love the game. This is their loss.

TOP TIP

The umpire is always right. Even when the replay proves that he is an idiot.

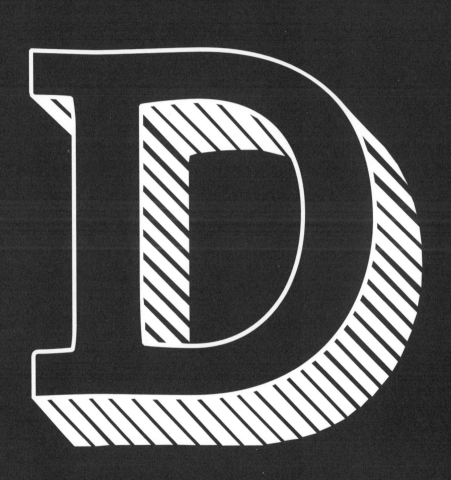

DARTS

When you are sat in a pub watching two drunk, overweight men throwing tungsten arrows at a board, it may stun you to discover that this is not a pastime, it is a sport. Not only is it a sport, it is one taken seriously by thousands of fans across the country, with tickets to major tournaments selling out in minutes.

If you are lucky enough to get tickets to a tournament, what you are actually attending is the closest thing Britain has to Oktoberfest. Spectators arrive drunk and leave comatose, having spent a few hours largely oblivious to the skill levels of the actual players, so in thrall are they to the joys of overpriced, watered-down beer. This is a world where a man can earn the nickname 'Crafty' without having shown any evidence of guile whatsoever. It should be experienced at least once.

PRACTICE QUESTION

What is the ideal way to finish 166 in three darts?

DEVOLUTION

Yes, it is called the United Kingdom. But right now it is neither. In 2014, an increasingly fractious debate took place in which the nation of Scotland had a vote on self-government. On the one hand, the nationalists explained that the home of John Logie Baird, Alexander Fleming and the Krankies, of lorne sausage, deep-fried confectionery and a hell of a lot of oil should have the confidence to go it alone.

TOP TIP

Don't get involved.

On the other hand, the Better Together campaigners said, 'This is all a bit much isn't it? I'm scared.' Mel Gibson's opinion was not sought.

Meanwhile, the English just wanted to stay mates, not least because the prospect of finding the best tennis player in England was too depressing to contemplate.

The terrified ones won the vote. England breathed a sigh of relief. But that sense of relief was short-lived. In May 2015, a resurgence of Scottish nationalism saw sensational General Election triumphs, transforming Nicola Sturgeon into a political superstar, and setting new challenges for Westminster's chefs. What the immediate future holds is, quite frankly, anyone's guess.

A
B
C
D
E
F
G
H
I
J
K
L
M
N
O
P
Q
R
S
T
U
V
W
X
Y
Z

GAY AND LESBIAN

Times have changed. Once upon a time Britain exported repressive homophobic laws around the world. Uganda and India may not have moved on, but Britain has, and is now more gay-friendly than Paul Ross having a midlife crisis. Here are some useful pieces of advice.

1 That air steward you spotted on your flight over here? He is.

2 If you have seen someone you like, try the traditional British gay chat-up lines: What's your name? Where are you from? What constituency do you represent?

3 If you are a lesbian, you could try a complicated and stressful coming-out process. Or alternatively, you could move to the West Yorkshire market town of Hebden Bridge. The same result is achieved.

4 If your musical tastes include the Rolling Stones, David Bowie, Radiohead and the Arctic Monkeys, then the gay scene is possibly not for you. If you think that the group Steps represents the zenith of musical history, you will be in your element.

5 Attitudes do differ around the country. Central Manchester, central London (with the exception of Regent's Park Mosque) and central Liverpool all have a deeply ingrained gay scene. Birmingham has its moments, and pretty much everyone in Brighton has dabbled. If you live in Plymouth or Sunderland, however, stay at home and use the Internet or a gender-specific smartphone app. It is much safer.

6 Just because you can get married, it does not mean that you have to. It is a big and expensive commitment. Think long and hard.

7 Adopting an über-camp persona places you at the front of the queue for game shows and miscellaneous reality television.

 Avoid John Barrowman.

PRINCESS DIANA

Nobody feels comfortable about the untimely death of beautiful women. In modern times, Britain has not reacted en masse to any world event to the degree that they mourned the most famous of the victims of a high-speed car crash in Paris, in August 1997.

Before the crash, Diana was a much derided, flighty figure of fun. Afterwards, her reputation rapidly ascended into near sainthood as a nation grieved like it had never grieved before. Elton John hastily reworked one of his worst songs as a tribute, and it became the best-selling UK single of all time. To this day, it is hard to say whether this was an appropriate response, or a terrifying overreaction. But you do need to know that for a few weeks in the autumn of 1997, Britain had a collective soul.

TOP TIP

Buy one of Elton John's early albums. You will be pleasantly surprised at how good it is.

CHARLES DICKENS

During your time in Britain, you will meet people who nostalgically hark back to the values of Victorian Britain, which they believe represented a golden era in our history. As the works of Britain's most celebrated novelist will attest, the truth is a lot more complicated. It was indeed the best of times for some, and the very worst of times for many more.

It is easy to forget the degree to which Charles Dickens traded in human misery. Children take regular beatings, evil step-uncles connive, the rich continually fleece the poor and a number of the characters perish through consumption or, in one notable case, spontaneous combustion. It is not a joyous carnival of entertainment, but it is undoubtedly well-written and wise.

Read one of the novels just to claim that you have, or alternatively watch the film musical *Oliver!*, which covers similar ground to Dickens but with much better songs.

PRACTICE QUESTION

Explain the plot of *Bleak House* without hesitation, deviation or repetition.

DOCTOR WHO

It is hard to know where to begin with this entertainment behemoth. In 1963, one day after the assassination of JFK, the BBC broadcast their new drama series, a somewhat creaky affair about an eccentric time traveller. One thing rather led to another, and 52 years later it is one of the BBC's biggest global success stories.

The quality has varied wildly, as the Doctor has regenerated again and again into a slightly different middle-class white man. But one thing has remained constant. *Doctor Who* fanatics, of whom there are hundreds of thousands, are an insufferable bunch, who spend their lives scoring points off each other about who said what to whom and why in the episode 'Revenge of the Technoroboticons'.

Watching *Doctor Who* fanatics communicate with each other is much like watching chimpanzees communicate with each other – if you look carefully enough and for long enough they start to resemble real people.

This is a shame, because it is actually a warm, clever show. Watch it, just keep your thoughts about it to yourself.

PRACTICE QUESTION

Formulate a hypothetical series of circumstances that could result in the casting of a black actor as the Doctor.

DOWNTON ABBEY

And so, by a quirk of alphabetical listing, we move straight on to another of Britain's great TV exports. I can't imagine that anyone truly foresaw the scale of its success when writer Julian Fellowes first turned up at ITV and said 'You know what? I don't think Sunday night telly is quite posh enough yet.'

Thus it came to pass that a monster was born. A slick, clichéd all-consuming monster. Please don't make the mistake of thinking that one day this lifestyle could be your lifestyle. Even if you win the lottery, it won't be. It is an idealised version of Britain designed to play into the hands of the US television market, whose viewers still believe many of us lead these lives. It is part of the great British tradition that on Sunday evenings television should hark back to yesteryear. And annoyingly, Downton Abbey does it rather well.

TOP TIP

These people may have had servants, but it was a very different era. Do not start getting any ideas.

DRIVING

You don't have to be a driver to live here. But it helps.

If you live in a big city, then perhaps you are right to consider car ownership a luxury. But for most people, the ability to get from A to B in a journey whose small pleasures have been destroyed by temporary roadworks is an absolute necessity.

The driving test may seem daunting, but a quick glance at just how many prize pillocks have passed the test should tell you that this is one exam that you should be able to pass eventually.

The harder task is to keep your sanity once you have passed your test. Driving on the M6 and the M25 at any time approaching peak hours is a brutal mental and physical endurance test that no person should ever have to face. Turn on the traffic news on any Friday, and it appears that the entire nation has come to a catastrophic standstill. In addition, you will soon find out that every driver knows where the speed cameras are, except you.

> ## TOP TIP
>
> Eventually you will get done for doing 33mph in a 30mph zone, and you may be asked to attend a speed awareness course. Go. There are biscuits.

And you will also discover that the worst thing about driving is that you develop a hatred for all other drivers. Every other person sharing the road with you becomes a sworn enemy. This is usually utterly indefensible. But with bus drivers and taxi drivers, it tends to be pretty good character assessment.

So by all means pass your test, and buy a car. But I guarantee you that within months you will become a less patient, more intolerant human being.

EASTENDERS

In 2015, the BBC television soap opera *EastEnders* celebrated its 30th anniversary. In that time, members of its colourful cast of characters have been stabbed, raped, poisoned, blackmailed, beaten up, set on fire, buried alive, reincarnated and wed to Ian Beale.

One might think that this is an accurate reflection of life in East London. After all, who hasn't had an eleven-year-old neighbour accidentally murder his older sister with a jewellery box? But an accurate reflection, involving people living relatively uneventful lives, while cheerfully chatting to their Bangladeshi mates about local council corruption, would not make spectacular television.

My advice to you is this. Life is too short. An episode of *EastEnders* is so fixated on wallowing in the very depths of human misery, that I can't help thinking that there are better ways of spending half an hour of your life. Walk the dog. If you don't have a dog, walk someone else's. Write an angry letter to your MP. Do anything other than watch an episode of *EastEnders*. Thirty minutes in its unhappy company will make the lure of antidepressants seem irresistible.

PRACTICE QUESTION

Nick Cotton is definitely dead. Describe three scenarios in which the producers could credibly bring him back to life.

EDINBURGH

There are many things in Britain that can be described as beautiful. A David Gower cover drive, a freshly made bacon sandwich, the tears of a child knocked out of *Britain's Got Talent* (see page 33).

But nothing quite prepares you for your first visit to Edinburgh. It sure is pretty. Edinburgh is Glasgow's big rival, an older, more elegant, more conservative sibling. Edinburgh is afternoon tea to Glasgow's afternoon lager. Its vistas are breathtaking, its pomp and sense of history all pervasive.

Or at least it is for eleven months of the year. In August it hosts the world's biggest arts festival. Edinburgh residents flee, cackling with delight that they have managed to rent out their three-bedroom flat for five grand for the month. Little do they know that when they return, their beloved flat is likely to have been ruined beyond all recognition by an overexcited trio of actors taking part in an all-male production of *The Merry Husbands of Windsor*.

The price of everything in Edinburgh during August is a disgrace, and only visit if you have somewhere to stay. If you do visit you will be rewarded with cultural riches, and performers who range from brilliant to street entertainer. And do make sure you take the opportunity to see the city outside of August, because Edinburgh is, literally, Britain's most beautiful city.

A
B
C
D
E
F
G
H
I
J
K
L
M
N
O
P
Q
R
S
T
U
V
W
X
Y
Z

TOP TIP

Edinburgh's drinking scene is not as fierce as Glasgow's. Nonetheless, don't ask anyone about devolution.

ENGLISH DEFENCE LEAGUE

Britain has among its population a number of Islamic extremists. Of this there can be little doubt. Exactly what the scale of the problem is can be debated, and I don't have any clear ideas about what the best course of action might be. But I am pretty sure that the answer isn't to join the emotionally stunted, paramilitary wing of far-right activism that is the English Defence League.

Formed from the splinters of football hooliganism, the English Defence League is PATRIOTIC. In fact, their members love their country so much, they enjoy disfiguring its town and city centres on Saturday afternoons.

'Not all EDL members are stupid or violent', they protest. Well, not all Muslims are stupid or violent either, but the EDL steadfastly refuses to see the irony. But then, some of their members venerate the war dead *and* make Nazi salutes. History is not their strong point.

To be honest, the English Defence League is probably an unattractive prospect to a new immigrant. I am simply making you aware of its existence.

EUROPEAN UNION

A
B
C
D
E
F
G
H
I
J
K
L
M
N
O
P
Q
R
S
T
U
V
W
X
Y
Z

You may be surprised to discover just how many laws you subscribe to as a UK resident are actually made in Brussels. In 1973, Britain agreed to enter what was then a relatively small-scale trade agreement. Now few seem to know quite what to do about the fact that the European Union is both massive, and massively powerful.

UKIP, and its 'charismatic' leader Nigel Farage, have gained much political momentum by tapping into the traditional British distrust of the rest of Europe. At the time of writing I have no idea how close the nation is to an epoch-defining referendum. Your best option is to do what the rest of us do. Keep your fingers crossed and hope everything is going to be okay.

TOP TIP

Unrestricted travel
within the EU? You
would be mad not to
take advantage.
I'll meet you at the
Louvre for lunch.

FISH AND CHIPS

It is part of the genius of Britain that it has taken a commonly held belief, that seafood is healthy, and created a version of seafood for which the absolute opposite is true.

Fish and chips is the national dish of Britain. Others make similar claims for chicken tikka masala, but this is arrant nonsense. It is fish and chips that is truly loved by people across every demographic group, and is perhaps the origin of the much-heard phrase, 'Yes I am a vegetarian, but I do occasionally eat fish.'

After all, who could resist? Battered cod, haddock, or plaice, with deep-fried, chunky, flavoursome chipped potatoes – to be honest, I am getting ravenous just writing these words. An added advantage is that you have the food in your hands within minutes of ordering. In a newspaper. Finally, someone has found a use for the *Daily Star*.

Like all truly great foods, it represents terrible news for your arteries. So I would advise that you don't have the dish any more than four times a day. But you have to try it. I will reluctantly make an exception for people who have ethical reasons for not eating fish. But for the rest of you, if you haven't done fish and chips, you are a long way from citizenship.

TOP TIP

No good has ever come of ordering that sausage in batter.

FOX HUNTING

'The unspeakable in full pursuit of the uneatable'. Oscar Wilde was by no means perfect, but on this subject, he was spot on. I am not an expert on rural matters and am prepared to accept that foxes are an enormous nuisance to people living in farming communities.

This does not mean there cannot be a more elegant way to deal with the problem than to create a ritualistic festival of bloodthirsty carnage. As an immigrant, this probably does not concern you, in that it is very unlikely that your face will fit in this particular niche of society for a few decades yet. But you need to know that those wild animals that you see wandering alone at night in urban areas, the ones you probably think are quite cute, are actually seen by farmers as their mortal enemy. Along with lefties and vegans.

And you need to know that what might seem like an unnecessarily brutal, smug and celebratory way to deal with a pest is actually seen by certain communities as the very height of living.

TOP TIP

Do you have your own pest to deal with? Just dress up select members of your own neighbourhood in bizarre garb and go on a frenzied and violent 'Hunt for the housefly'.

FRANCE

Yes, Britain has a long rivalry with Germany, but it's one that is tinged with a slight degree of respect, and envy at the strength of their economy. No such respect or envy exists when it comes to the rivalry with France. We won at Crécy. We won at Agincourt. We won at Trafalgar and at Waterloo. We didn't collaborate with the Nazis. So how is it that *they* are the ones with the arrogant sense of cultural superiority?

Yes, there are things that the French have done well. Renaissance art and architecture. Fast trains. Daft Punk.

But they have not really achieved enough to justify the haughty contempt that they have for other nations, which reached its nadir in 2005 when the then President, Jacques Chirac, in a desperate attempt to derail London's bid to clinch the 2012 Summer Olympics (see page 122), openly criticised the quality of British food.

British food has its ups and its downs. But they are mostly ups. As a nation we would never find ourselves dismembering frogs, or smothering snails in garlic in a grim manoeuvre to try to make them remotely palatable. And what is more, in Britain the far right are a deservedly mocked political force with no influence whatsoever. The French electorate once came perilously close to electing Jean-Marie Le Pen as President.

> ## PRACTICE QUESTION
> Why would a nation with the most ethnically diverse football team in history ever vote National Front?

For all that, there are some lovely places in France that are well worth a visit. Just don't get any ideas about living there. The French are far less immigrant-friendly than the British.

GERMANY

Along with France (see page 68), Germany remains Britain's bitterest rival. Between the years 1939 and 1945 Britain provided heroic resistance against the Nazis in a war that was unusual, in that the British were, undeniably and unequivocally, the good guys. Germany had lost their collective minds and Britain does not want them to forget it.

This is because since unification, the citizens of Germany have gone from strength to smug, self-confident strength with a sense of national identity that allows them to simply not give a damn about 1966. They are perfectly happy making great cars and terrible music. So take every opportunity in life to let a German know that you have never, and will never, forget.

> **PRACTICE QUESTION**
>
> Explain in less than 300 words how the nation that produced Goethe, Einstein and Brecht also wholly embraced the music of David Hasselhoff.

GLASGOW

It is the opinion of the author that Glasgow is one of the greatest cities on earth, and that is despite having had a complete stranger punch me in the face while I was patiently waiting for a chicken shish kebab in a Glaswegian takeaway. You need to ignore the occasional stench of sectarian hatred, often fuelled by the obsessional support for two very bad football teams.

You need to ignore the dreary climate, the cholesterol-tastic diet, and the fact that Glaswegians use the 'c' word as a term of endearment. Instead, celebrate the superb architecture, late-night Chinese restaurants on Sauchiehall Street and most of all, the relentless drinking culture. Drinking with Glaswegians is like playing football with Cristiano Ronaldo. You are lucky to be doing it with the finest practitioners of the art in the world. Apart from the guy who punched me in the face. He is a prick.

TOP TIP

I'm not exaggerating. Glasgow is a great city. Just don't venture too far out of the centre unless you have a Glaswegian local to guide you.

GLASTONBURY

I am aware that many immigrants have escaped horrific living conditions in their own countries. To those who fall into this category, the last thing I would do is recommend spending hundreds of pounds to recreate those conditions by going to the Glastonbury Festival. The only difference between the two being that at Glastonbury, from about half a mile away, you might be able to see the band London Grammar.

To a lot of people half my age, it is a magical experience, one that they will partially remember and eulogise over for decades to come. I am not a curmudgeon and I wish these young people well. But frankly I would rather take a cheese grater to my nether regions than put myself through it. And I love music, but I also love comfort, not wallowing in mud and the unrestricted use of flush toilets.

PRACTICE QUESTION

Name three bands that it would be worth paying hundreds of pounds to get a slight glimpse of.

There is no doubt that, musically, Glastonbury is one of the greatest festivals the world has to offer. Stay in, watch the BBC coverage with a takeaway pizza, a glass of wine and access to your very own bathroom. Leave the festival to the youngsters.

GOLF

In 1457, James II of Scotland banned golf as an unwelcome distraction from archery. Perhaps he had the right idea. There is nothing wrong with the sport *per se*, though how the art of using a stick to hit a ball into a hole became a multimillion-dollar sporting success story is anyone's guess.

It is just that the golf club has come to represent much that is wrong with society. A stiflingly conservative place where business deals are sealed in the clubhouse, UKIP councillors decry immigration while negotiating bunkers, and women know their place.

That is the image that I have, anyway. Perhaps it is an ignorant one, but after I was thrown off a golf course in Dulwich in 1985 for wearing the wrong kind of trousers, I have never had much desire to return. As a newcomer, you may crave golf club membership as a symbol of your improved social standing. The truth is that it will be many, many years before you represent the kind of member that the committee is looking for.

TOP TIP

Try crazy golf instead. It is a pacier, more entertaining version of the real thing with no membership criteria whatsoever...and with more windmills.

FOOTBALL

It is possible to live a full life in Britain while taking not the slightest interest in football, but there is no point in pursuing such a potentially difficult course of action. Even at the most middle-class of dinner parties, conversation will inevitably turn to Britain's national game. If you are a woman, or an openly gay man, society has assumed that you will have no practical knowledge of the game. This does not have to be the case. It is not that difficult to turn yourself from footballing ignoramus to the Yoda of the offside rule. Here are the basics.

1 England won the World Cup in 1966. They had the benefit of home advantage, and a dodgy Russian linesman. But they won. And they have never shut up about it, because the national record since then has been one of disappointment and progressive incompetence.

2 The other home nations, particularly the Scots, loathe England with an indefatigable passion. Sadly, although Wales, Scotland and Northern Ireland have all had their moments, their national teams have failed to make an impact in recent years. If you are English and find yourself in a Scottish football conversation, either a) pretend to be mute or b) say, 'Archie Gemmill's goal against Holland has to be the greatest goal of all time.'

3 Football manager is the only skilled occupation in the world that the average Brit thinks he can do better than the fully qualified man who currently does the job. For your own safety, simply indulge that Brit. Don't say 'What would you know? You don't even have any basic coaching qualifications.' Do say, 'Yep, Mike, you are spot on.'

4 I speak as a Londoner who has supported Liverpool FC all his life. Pick a local club to support. More than anything else you owe it to your kids to give them a bond to their local community. It certainly helps with integration.

5 When international tournaments come round, set your expectations low. Don't put a flag on your car – when your country is eliminated you will forget to take it down and look like a pillock. You are not going to win. Ever. It will be Germany or Spain yet again. There is a reason why nobody buys bad World Cup songs any more – people have got used to the fact that hope is an extremely cruel mistress.

6 Don't tweet Joey Barton. You will still be engaged in the argument six months later. The man can hold a grudge.

7 Sometimes you may be offered tickets to see your team, but it is in the other team's stand. You might think you have the skills to sit in that stand and not give the game away. You haven't. Do not do it, it is not worth the risk to life and limb.

8 Luckily, the amount of time it takes for Robbie Savage to explain himself on *Match of the Day* is the exact amount of time required to make a nice cup of tea.

9 If you support a team owned by a Russian oligarch or an Arab oil baron, you have not earned the right to be shocked when your club makes inexplicable business decisions.

Football can be an ugly pastime. Horrible human beings are worshipped unconditionally, it often lacks any kind of ethical code. A lot of perpetually angry bigots love football, and love abusing anyone who plays badly, or plays well for the opposing team. But at its heart, football is the most popular team sport in the world, a game of breathtaking theatre and wondrous human achievement. And it was invented in Britain. Don't watch with anger and hate. Live and breathe a brilliant sport – believe me, your kids will be undyingly grateful to you for introducing them to it.

GRAND NATIONAL

For one Saturday in April every year, the eyes of the nation turn to Aintree for the equine version of *The Hunger Games*. Forty horses start what has become known as the 'world's greatest steeplechase'. Some will never make it to Sunday.

It is by far the biggest betting event of the year. Even those whose religion clearly forbids gambling will slip down to Ladbrokes for a furtive bet on an Irish, lightly raced nine-year-old that has been bred to stay 4½ miles.

The ten-minute spectacle is brutal and exhilarating in equal measure, as punters desperately struggle to find out if their selected horse is challenging for the lead, or halfway to the glue factory.

Legends are made, dreams are crushed, and for a select group of gamblers, drinks are very much on them. Place a bet, enjoy the spectacle, and hope against hope that, after the race, your wallet will be just that little bit more stuffed. Or boycott the whole farrago in protest at the inherent cruelty of it all. Either way, you won't be judged.

> ## TOP TIP
>
> If the horse has run well at the most recent Cheltenham Festival, then he or she will not have the legs to win the Grand National. Place your bet elsewhere.

GREAT BRITISH BAKE OFF

Television has an important part to play in cultural integration. Discussing last night's telly by the water-cooler is a great way of bonding with your work colleagues. Bizarrely, the one programme which provokes the most debate involves watching a group of polite, impeccably behaved people attempting to make a Sachertorte.

The Great British Bake Off is testament to the fact that with a bit of luck and a fair wind, just about anything can become a cultural phenomenon. Each episode is about 20 minutes too long, and Sue Perkins and the other one do not add a huge amount to the proceedings. It is a world where a misplaced Baked Alaska represents the biggest scandal since Watergate.

TOP TIP

Good supermarkets provide excellent ready-made cakes and pastries.

It is a world where 'Hollywood sex symbol' does not refer to an icon from the golden age of cinema, but to a silver-haired Liverpudlian elbows deep in yeast. The treat 'em mean, keep 'em keen Paul Hollywood finds his perfect foil in fellow judge Mary Berry, a woman whose benign presence and baking expertise has her challenging the Queen for Britain's favourite grandma. There is no doubt that the viewers are gripped, I suspect pleasantly surprised by a group of contestants who are not the usual needy, whorish reality show wannabes.

So just sit back and enjoy a bunch of lovely people creating cakes and pastries of a quality you can only ever dream of achieving.

GREGGS

Seemingly at the polar opposite end of the baking social spectrum is Greggs, a hugely successful, ubiquitous feature of virtually every high street. Like Argos (see page 17), Greggs is perhaps best known for the middle-class sneer, the refusal to countenance the idea that anyone would willingly be seen dead in there.

Well let them sneer. I am middle class. I love cricket, and have once been at a party with Gyles Brandreth. And I adore Greggs. There is a reason for its success, and the reason is simple: it makes okay food at extremely accessible prices.

Lunch does not have to be fancy. Sometimes there is a medium-sized hole in your stomach. And sometimes that hole can best be filled by a Steak Bake. The snobs can fulminate all they like. The truth is, at many Greggs up and down the country queues for the food stretch way out into the street. It is definitely doing something right.

PRACTICE QUESTION

If you have decided to lunch at Greggs, how much change will you have from £2?

GYM MEMBERSHIP

Don't do it. If you really are an obsessive bodybuilder with a desire to lift weights, then join. But for everyone else, don't do it.

Exercise is obviously a good thing. But don't join a gym. Go for a brisk walk, or a run. Pay a lot less to occasionally use your local swimming baths. Raise your heart rate by watching *Question Time*. But gym membership? Don't do it.

Gym membership preys on the delusion that once we join a gym we will go every week. It never works out like that. Life is too busy and complicated. Then we sit around not knowing how to cancel the deal. 'Maybe I will give it a couple more months, see if I go to the gym more often'. It never happens. And so you try to cut short your gym membership. That is when the horrors begin.

Incorporated into your contract are any number of clauses that render you financially impotent should you choose to leave. When they presented the contract to you, they caught you at your most idealistic, stupidly naïve, vulnerable moment. This is your fault. You did not read the contract, nor think too hard about the consequences of signing it.

TOP TIP

Don't do it.

So instead of leaving, you cling on to the 100–1 shot that one day you will rediscover some enthusiasm for the tedium of the treadmill. You never will.

The plus side is that you may end up losing weight because you can no longer afford to buy food.

HARRY POTTER

(Takes off curmudgeon's hat and begins to write).

Every so often, somebody from Britain metaphorically conquers the world. It might be musical geniuses like The Beatles (see page 25), or a TV show like *Downton Abbey* (see page 57).

Then there is the case of the down-at-heel writer called Joanne, who concocted a harmless book about a boy wizard, changed her name from Joanne to J.K. so as not to put off misogynist wizard lovers, and promptly changed the course of publishing history.

I will be honest, I do not get it. I don't care about magic owls, and broomsticks and goblets of fire. I am 45 years old. I am sure it is very well written, but it is definitely not for me.

But you should care. Your kids need to mix with other kids. And other kids are obsessed with Harry Potter. They know everything in Rowling's richly populated fantasy world: from Aragog, the giant spider in the Forbidden Forest, to the goblins of Gringott's Bank, right through to Zonko's Joke Shop. If your kids want to fit in, they need to get with the Harry Potter plan. You don't have to read the books or watch the films. You're better than that. But your kids do.

TOP TIP

Britain has many bookshops selling novels written with adults in mind, some of them by J.K. Rowling. Try these instead.

HEN NIGHTS

A hen night is a monumental occasion, an opportunity for a prospective bride to get together with her friends and enjoy one last night of symbolic freedom. And there can be no better way to celebrate that than an evening of sophistication, in which the bride dresses up in a tatty imitation of a wedding dress, with a 'learner' plate stuck on her back, while the others brandish inflatable penises around town.

If executed perfectly, the British hen night may well be the worst sociocultural monstrosity on the planet. The idea of pacing the alcohol intake has long been killed off, as a series of flaming sambucas and Jägerbombs renders the group incapable of anything remotely resembling social interaction.

Pity the limousine driver, who once dreamt of chauffeuring George Clooney to a film première, but is now reduced to ferrying around a collection of shrieking drunks, one of whom is unconscious, one of whom is covered in her own sick, and one of whom is waving an inflatable penis through the limousine's sun roof.

Come, friendly bombs, and fall on whichever late-night venue they are in.

PRACTICE QUESTION

1. Calculate the number of units of alcohol in a flaming sambuca, and readjust your recommended speed of drinking accordingly.

2. List three reagents that can get vomit stains out of a dress in an emergency.

A
B
C
D
E
F
G
H
I
J
K
L
M
N
O
P
Q
R
S
T
U
V
W
X
Y
Z

HENRY VIII

Henry VIII represents the very selective manner with which Britain views history. A walk around beautiful Hampton Court Palace comes highly recommended, its exquisite architecture and surrounds conjuring up evocative images of what Tudor life must have been like.

What the tour guide will neglect to say, however, is that Henry VIII was a philandering sociopath whose attitude towards his opponents was far more 'beheady' than strictly necessary. The man who established the Church of England in its most modern sense did so in a fit of pique in order to get a divorce from his first wife, Catherine of Aragon. For Catherine of Aragon, this was actually a mighty fine result, given that two further wives lost their heads for spurious reasons. A long time before #everydaysexism, Henry VIII was writing the rule book on it.

> ## TOP TIP
> Don't enter Hampton Court maze unless you have a far better sense of direction than me. That was one helicopter rescue that I will never live down.

So when anyone claims that students no longer know enough about Britain's great history, ask him (it is always a him), 'Do you consider double uxoricide to be great?'

HOTELS

The good news is that Britain has hotels for every budget, and decent three- or four-star hotels can be surprisingly affordable. The exception to this is in London. Never stay in London unless you have friends to stay with or you are earning a fortune. In London, two hundred pounds gets you a shared room with eleven backpackers, three of whom snore like pigs.

As with so much in life, when you are trying to book a hotel, the Internet is your friend. Go to TripAdvisor to read reviews that are either from honest tourists or dishonest rivals. By ignoring the best and worst reviews, you should be able to get a decent idea of what the hotel is like. Chain hotels may be soulless but you know exactly what you are getting, and you may bump into Lenny Henry. He loves them.

If you are planning to stay in major cities, book as early as possible. Sometimes big sports events or rock concerts are taking place that massively reduce availability. During the 2002 Commonwealth Games in Manchester, I had to stay for two nights in Oldham. Never again.

Some hotels overcharge for Wi-Fi. Avoid them like the plague. Also, if anyone cheerfully informs you that you *can* get Wi-Fi in the hotel reception area, they clearly have no idea why you might need Internet access.

TOP TIP

Bring your own extension cable. You will be surprised to know how few hotels have sockets next to the bed.

I'M A CELEBRITY GET ME OUT OF HERE!

Once upon a time, Britain used to ridicule the low-quality programming from the rest of the world, and in particular, laugh at the unfathomably weird challenges on Japanese game shows. These days, I suspect that the Japanese look at us and wonder to themselves, 'Why is Edwina Currie eating a kangaroo testicle? I expected better from her. Not a lot better. But better.'

Personally, I cannot see the purpose of dragging together a diverse group of people united only by their need for the limelight and their lack of self-respect. Instead of displaying the very skills and talent that made them famous in the first place, they become the victims of an increasingly macabre set of tasks. Like the Romans in the Colosseum, we watch in large numbers, hoping that the humiliations will be memorable. Shame on us and our need to enjoy our own lives via the suffering of others. The prize is a mild raising of their celebrity profile, and the occasional extra appearance on *Loose Women*.

The show, like all the shows featured in this guide, is hugely popular. Draw your own conclusions.

PRACTICE QUESTION

What does Christopher Biggins actually do?

INDIA

Back in the 18th century, Britain looked at a far off land of spices and thought to itself, 'I'm having that'. In 1947, after 190 years of British rule, India threw off the shackles, became independent and collectively said, 'Right. How about this time *we* come and visit *you?*'

Thus began a pattern of immigration that explains why there are Indian/Pakistani restaurants seemingly everywhere in Britain, and why thousands of young club cricketers can now bowl leg spin. It is also why this book exists, my parents having arrived here in 1968, with, as the dinner party anecdote goes, just £1.50 in their pockets.

I am not going to be naïve and complacent and say that it has been all plain sailing. Not all of the indigenous population are cheering wildly about the project, and certain rather preachy members of the Asian community are about as interested in social cohesion as I am in Harry Potter. But it cannot be denied that the Indian restaurant remains a business triumph, and its ubiquity quite extraordinary.

I don't dine much at Indian restaurants for the predictable reason that my Mum's cooking is much better. But my top tips still come from decades of experience.

TOP TIPS

1. Never be rude to the waiters. Their revenge will be horrific.

2. Rice is fine. But it is foolish to miss the opportunity to eat freshly made bread.

3. Indian food is full of rich, nuanced flavours. These are all obliterated by the spices of a vindaloo. Order one and you'll get no sympathy from me.

4. Chicken tikka masala is a perfectly adequate dish, but it is for people too timid to try actual Indian food.

5. There are times when paying that little bit extra for quality toilet paper certainly pays off.

A
B
C
D
E
F
G
H
I
J
K
L
M
N
O
P
Q
R
S
T
U
V
W
X
Y
Z

NEWSPAPERS

You can try as hard as you like to get all your news from the Internet, but sooner or later, you are going to have to make occasional use of newspapers. Luckily, local newspapers are often delivered to your door, giving you essential information about a church fête, a wheelie bin that blew over, or a man who injured his finger in an accident with a barbecue.

To assess the state of the nation, however, you do need the national press. Their journalists are news-gatherers, gossipmongers and phone hackers, living by a moral code which varies from hypocritical to non-existent. The sales of newspapers may be in declining health, but they remain very important. We shall look at them in descending order of daily circulation.

The king of them all is **THE SUN**. Owned by a preening pantomime villain, it has always won the circulation war by only caring about one thing – winning the circulation war. So it gives the public what it wants; lies, brutally honest football reports and bare-chested women. The public are well aware that *The Sun* has a distinctly erratic relationship with the truth, but its bluntness and clarity of message has enabled it to enjoy 'market leader' status for a number of years. I would never buy it, I support Liverpool FC. If you really must read it, visit your local café or Chinese takeaway.

Even more depressingly, the only other paper to rival *The Sun* for circulation is the **DAILY MAIL**. As an immigrant, only read this paper if you are of a hardy disposition. Because the *Daily Mail* hates you. Don't worry too much though, you are certainly not alone. You are on a list that includes working women, fat women, thin women, homosexuals, lefties, eco-activists, anyone who wasn't on Hitler's side in the 1930s, anyone with a comprehensive school education, all members of the Afro-Caribbean diaspora, and Ed Miliband's Dad. It is an illustrious list; be proud if you are on it. Do not *buy* this putrid paper. If you are that desperate to read about the presence of a Kardashian at a fashion show, then look the story up online.

The **DAILY MIRROR** purports to be the big rival to *The Sun*, but possesses neither its humour nor its relentless sense of evil. It doesn't quite have the nerve to be truly nasty, and as a result lacks a clearly defined identity. And many have never forgiven it for the Piers Morgan years. The *Daily Mirror* remains the paper of choice for those who want their drivel written from a more leftist perspective.

THE DAILY TELEGRAPH represents the golf-club face of conservatism. To paraphrase Mark Twain, it is very much the *Daily Mail* with a college education. With its reverence for royalty, class discrimination and the public school system, it is, perhaps, a surprising choice as Britain's most popular broadsheet newspaper. It may be that the quality of the writing successfully hides its lack of inclusivity.

If anything, the **DAILY EXPRESS** has taken the *Daily Mail*'s formula and made it even more crude. Its famous obsession with ludicrous Princess Diana conspiracy theories has perhaps fatally damaged its reputation.

The *DAILY STAR* attempts to simplify *The Sun*'s formula. It is barely coherent nonsense, and only bought by people unfortunate enough to find themselves at the lower end of the literacy scale.

Owned by the same villain who owns *The Sun*, **THE TIMES** is the Grandaddy of British daily newspapers. It eschews sensationalist headlines for high-quality journalism, and wears its political allegiances lightly. It has superlative sports coverage, a world-famous daily crossword and Sudokus to die for. It says much about the dumbing down of mainstream British life that every day, more people buy the *Daily Star* than *The Times*. Contemplate that fact and weep.

A few years ago, **THE INDEPENDENT** realised that its brand of worthy journalism was failing to catch the public imagination, and launched a sister paper called the *i*, a title designed for the hard of spelling. Presenting the same stories, with shorter words and larger pictures, has seen a resurgence in a once-failing brand. Unfortunately, sales figures for the older sibling remain pitiful. The public appetite for reading about complex issues remains limited.

It is possibly a victim of its own high-quality website, but nobody seems to buy **THE GUARDIAN** any more. Perhaps its target audience of hipsters and hippies, gay theatre lovers, and earnest political activists has simply moved on to imbibing news via the latest apps and gadgets. Whatever the reason, *The Guardian*'s very distinct brand of methodically chosen news reporting has an appeal that dwindles with every passing month. When people sneer at 'Guardianistas', they should be aware that whoever it is they are mocking is statistically more likely to be a reader of the *i*.

So in summary, never buy *The Sun* or the *Daily Mail*. If your politics lean to the left, buy the *i*. If your politics lean to the right, buy *The Times*. And if all you want is to ogle big-breasted ladies, then stop reading this book, and get yourself onto the World Wide Web.

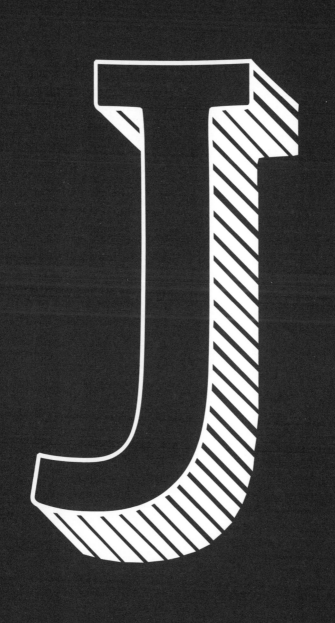

BORIS JOHNSON

British politics is a complex beast, and at the time of writing, it was about to get even more complicated. But most things you need to know about the British attitude to politics can be encapsulated by a look at the career of Boris Johnson.

By any criteria, Johnson is a cartoonish buffoon. Born into privilege and educated at Eton, it was certainly no surprise that during his Oxford University years, he found himself a fully fledged member of the Bullingdon Club. Given that this was a most dislikeable set of port-swilling hooligans, characterised by their members' utter contempt for those deemed socially inferior, this could be seen as a regrettable career move.

Add to this his track record of political bumbling, social faux pas and adultery, and you might think that 'BoJo' is unpopular. But British politics does not work like that. British politics is so stuffed with dull, careerist automatons and yes-men who wouldn't know the price of a pint of milk if their lives depended on it that Boris Johnson has become the most popular politician in Britain by simply offering something different from the norm. His pratfalls are celebrated, his faux pas merely spun into something loveable and cuddly.

> ## PRACTICE QUESTION
>
> Name one occasion when Boris Johnson exhibited wisdom and insight.

That is British politics today. In such a sea of mediocrity, it is possible to become a Titan simply by not being boring. No wonder so many people love him. He looks hilarious when stuck on a zip wire.

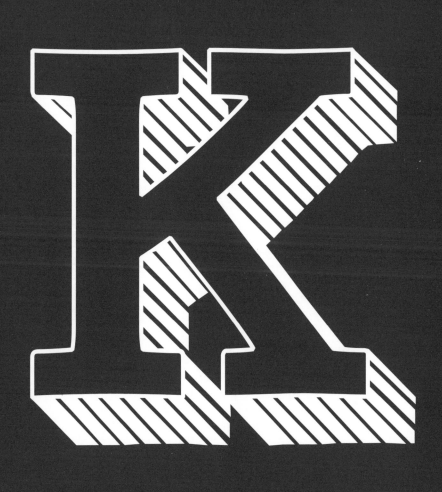

KEBAB SHOPS

They are everywhere. They are architecturally ugly, the service is perfunctory at best, and nobody ever builds an evening around one. But Britain's thousands of kebab shops serve a purpose as a reliable provider of food to hungry drunks. It really is only drunks who could walk into a kebab shop, look at the rotating slab of greased-up lamb and think, 'Yummy, yummy, yummy. That is exactly what my heart yearns for.'

The willingness of Britain's Turkish community to work into the small hours means that, for Britain's numerous drunks, the kebab shop is usually the final destination of the evening. As such, there is often an air of desperation, as men look around the shop searching for lone women who might be drunk enough to stop eating their chips and temporarily lower their standards. The real tragedy is the great missed opportunity that kebab shops offer. Doner kebabs are for the most part disgusting, but they are hugely popular due to the speed of service. If you are prepared to wait ten minutes, though, lamb and chicken shish kebabs are actually delicious. A bit more expensive than a doner, but it is actually proper, grilled food rather than ovine cast-offs.

> ### TOP TIP
> Never stop to think which parts of the sheep might be in a doner.

Unfortunately, Britain's drunks simply don't have that kind of patience, at that stage of inebriation and at that time of night. So be a maverick. Visit your local kebab shop in the afternoon or early evening. You will be pleasantly surprised at some of the treats that Turkish cuisine has to offer.

LEEDS

Leeds is the cultural and economic centre of a fiercely independent microstate called West Yorkshire. Despite the fact that the city and its surrounds have a reputation for being deeply suspicious of outsiders, especially southerners and Lancastrians, Leeds has much to admire.

It is a consumer's paradise. The entire centre of the city appears to be taken up by shops of every size and description, ranging from swanky boutiques (empty), to vast discount shops (very, very full).

It is also Britain's blokiest major city, driven by the twin obsessions of an underperforming football team and a far more successful Rugby League team. Pub conversation consists of little else.

Leeds is hard. It is surrounded by satellite towns that are even harder. The citizens of Halifax, Huddersfield *et al* make regular trips in, to enjoy unadulterated drinking. The chances are pretty high that you will see two men having a physical fight over the last Steak Bake in a late-night Greggs (see page 80). This represents theatre of the highest order, and it is with good reason that drunk students tend to avoid drunk civilians. Their relationship is not cosy.

> ## TOP TIP
>
> If you must go drinking in Leeds city centre, don't forget to bring your biggest, strongest mate.

Leeds is home to any number of superb restaurants, and England's most celebrated county cricket team, Yorkshire, best known around the world for Geoffrey Boycott. Boycott is more responsible than any other cricketer in history for the mistaken belief that cricket is boring.

LIVERPOOL

'Full of thieves and unemployment.' Thus begins and ends the most tedious of the stereotypes about Britain's most unfairly maligned city. It is true that Thatcherism was not kind to Merseyside, and signs of economic decline can be found all around.

But this is the city of The Beatles, Frankie Goes to Hollywood and Sonia. This is the city whose great rival football teams, Liverpool and Everton, have won five European Cups between them. In much the same way that Roger Federer and I have won seven Wimbledon titles between us.

Since Liverpool's shock nomination for 2008 European City of Culture, the city has rediscovered its *joie de vivre*. Where once, moustachioed men would terrify newcomers with their anachronistic stylings, now, well-dressed men and women sip lattes in upmarket cafés before sidling off to the new exhibition at the Walker Art Gallery. Dining options are diverse, one noted tapas restaurant serving mackerel semen. The vistas across the Mersey are as impressive as ever, and nothing stirs the soul more than the sight of an amphibious tourist vessel capsizing yet again. Best of all, you will never, ever find anyone reading a copy of *The Sun*.

> **PRACTICE QUESTION**
>
> Numerically and metaphorically, calculate the difference between 'Five European Cups' and 'Three European Cups'.

With as many bars, restaurants, museums and decent value hotels as anywhere, Liverpool is a great place to spend your time.

MADE IN CHELSEA

There is a stratum of society that you will never reach, unless the reason you are in the UK is because your Russian oligarch father has bought you a penthouse flat. You will never meet these people. You will never come across their work, because they have never had to work. They have never had to develop a personality, or learn how to make a cup of tea. All they have ever had to do is smile and quietly contemplate the good fortune of their colossally privileged upbringing.

Spiteful, bitter hatred is an extremely unattractive trait, and it is best not to make a habit of it. Yet it is undoubtedly wholly justified when watching the cast of the E4 reality show *Made in Chelsea*. Like *Big Brother*, this is a show to briefly scan, before forbidding your children from ever exhibiting any of the grotesque, vainglorious characteristics of the cast.

PRACTICE QUESTION

Name one single transferable skill possessed by any of these dimwits.

MANCHESTER

Given that it is a city with few obvious tourist attractions, it is greatly to Manchester's credit that it has emerged, culturally speaking, as England's second city. The reasons for this are diverse, and certainly start with the world's most famous football club and its deadly rival. The relentless success of these two clubs in recent years has won them fans from Abu Dhabi to Dubai.

Manchester is the most modern and progressive of cities, its 'Curry Mile' and gay village earning nationwide fame. Swish, upmarket bars, overlooking less swish canals, lure the punters in with the vague promise that there may be footballers drinking inside. Impressive Victorian architecture sits side by side with some of the most eye-catching new buildings Britain has to offer. The city has a rich comedy heritage, from the race-baiting of Bernard Manning to the more nuanced observations of current comedians about how people living in Didsbury are terribly middle-class.

More than all of this, Manchester has *swagger*. Mancunians are only too aware of their huge contribution to pop culture. After all, this is the city of The Smiths, Buzzcocks, Joy Division, New Order and Elbow. This is the city of Tony Wilson, Caroline Aherne and Steve Coogan. This is the city of the legendary 'Summer of Love', in which great dance music and ecstasy combined in thrilling fashion. Indeed, you are never that far away from survivors, men of a certain age, smiling and nodding their heads rhythmically, for whom it will always be 1989. So pack your bags and board that Pendolino train. You cannot fail to have fun in Manchester.

PRACTICE QUESTION

Man United or Man City? Which of these is the real Manchester club?

CHRISTMAS

Two thousand years ago, a hard-working carpenter and his heavily pregnant wife found accommodation difficult to come by and spent the night in a stable. The lack of coffee-making facilities and Wi-Fi caused a stress-induced labour, and the Son of God was born. Nobody knows for certain just which elements of this story are true. What is certain, though, is that Christmas is the biggest festival that the British celebrate. Here are some handy tips for surviving it.

1 Every January, stores offer discount prices on their goods. Buy your presents then. And feel defiantly smug for the rest of the year.

2 Frankincense, gold and myrrh are no longer appropriate Christmas gifts.

3 Try not to get too drunk at the work's Christmas party. The consequences of your misjudged sexual advances could prove catastrophic.

4 They say a second marriage is a triumph of hope over experience. The same goes for watching the Queen's Christmas message.

5 Boycott John Lewis. It is the only rational response to their appallingly saccharine, emotionally manipulative advertising campaigns.

6 For the other eleven months of the year do not eat parsnips. Then spend much of Christmas Day being pleasantly surprised at how delicious they are.

7 Vegetarians. If you have a day off, no one will judge you for it. A nut roast is not food. There is no need to suffer in silence.

8 Tell your kids that it's not Santa, it's you. One day they will be teenagers, and you will have completely forgotten what gratitude sounds like.

9 Your Dad can never have too many pairs of socks.

10 *Love Actually* is a terrible film. It contains the line 'At Christmas you tell the truth'. Nonsense. Do not tell the truth. Just remember that they are your relatives and you love them unconditionally. No good will come from telling the truth.

DAME HELEN MIRREN

See Dame Judi DENCH.

MRS BROWN'S BOYS

Laugh, and the whole world laughs with you. So to feel British, you need to laugh at what everybody else is laughing at. Fortunately, this is the land of P.G. Wodehouse, Tommy Cooper, Morecambe & Wise and a dog who could say 'sausages'.

But in terms of popularity, it seems that what makes Britain laugh more than anything else is an Irishman in a dress saying 'feck' quite a lot.

A great sitcom needs a cast of well-observed characters, great writing, engaging narratives and moments of pathos. *Mrs Brown's Boys* takes the rule book and rips it to shreds. It really offers none of these qualities, and yet the nation laughs along as though this was the funniest thing ever written.

I cannot explain it. Clearly the show wasn't made with me in mind. It was perhaps made for the benefit of people who work much harder than me, who when they relax, simply want entertainment that does not intellectually tax them in any way, and allows them, for a blissful half-hour, to forget their worries.

Mrs Brown's Boys makes a lot of people very happy indeed. To aid with cultural integration, perhaps it is just best not to fight it, sit back and laugh your head off. It is a bloke in a dress. What could be funnier than that?

TOP TIP

Don't be fooled by the language. 'Feck' is not an acceptable word to use in the workplace.

ANDY MURRAY

Don't be fooled by Wimbledon. For two weeks every summer, conversations turn to London SW19, and the high sporting drama contained therein. But Britain does not actually do tennis as such. Wimbledon itself is a two-tier disgrace, where genuine tennis fans have to queue overnight and corporate fans scoff extended lunches while their Centre Court seats remain unused. Try applying for a ticket yourself. Go on, I dare you.

Even now, tennis clubs maintain excellent facilities for their well-heeled members, while public courts maintain their state of disrepair. This sorry truth has led to British tennis becoming something of an international joke, and the reason Michael McIntyre and Jonathan Ross appear at Wimbledon so frequently is that they are currently Britain's eighth and ninth ranked male players.

It is out of this fog of utter mediocrity that a true British hero has emerged. He seems an unlikely hero, lacking the conventional handsomeness and easygoing charisma that

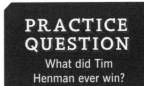

PRACTICE QUESTION
What did Tim Henman ever win?

so many sports stars have. His face usually contorted with frustration, anxiety or pain, he can be a difficult watch. The face of his Mum betrays the decades of hard graft she has put in to help her son achieve his goals. His mental state is fragile, especially compared to Federer, Nadal and Djokovic. And yet, for the last decade, Andy Murray has mixed it with his legendary rivals, occasionally come out on top, and provided Britain with its only tennis triumphs in living memory.

Britain has been spectacularly ungrateful to its only tennis superstar. His achievements are met with apathetic shrugs by much of the country, who don't like his demeanour, his Scottishness, his interviewing style and his second serve, but mainly don't like the fact that he is not a footballer.

After years of sacrifice and deserved success, all Andy Murray has to show for his career is a massive personal fortune, the unconditional love of his family and friends and a beautiful, if foul-mouthed, wife. But Britain is such a frustratingly cussed nation at times that he hasn't quite won over fickle Wimbledon fans. But then, despite hosting one of the world's great annual sports events, Britain doesn't really do tennis.

NATIONAL LOTTERY

You are allowed to dream. Who hasn't dreamt of a comfortable existence with no need to do any actual work ever again? It is a wonderful fantasy. Unfortunately, your statistical chances of winning are so remote that it is important not to let it take over your life.

The National Lottery serves a useful purpose. It helps fund worthwhile projects around the country, from bell-ringing classes for lesbians to major urban regeneration. It has certainly helped Dale Winton stay in the limelight. But you are not going to win. Remember that, and it is a harmless piece of escapism. There is a big difference between being a Saturday night dreamer and a slave to scratchcards.

TOP TIP

To try to get the most out of your lottery money, use the facilities and visit the towns and cities most helped by lottery funding. Also, when your numbers don't come in, look your partner in the eyes and say, 'I don't care. I have you. I have already won the lottery of life.' They will love you for it.

116

NEWCASTLE UPON TYNE

'Fog on the Tyne is all mine, all mine'.

The lyrics to Lindisfarne's Geordie anthem do not do justice to the majesty of one of Britain's great industrial cities. Newcastle, like its close relative Gateshead, is full of surprises. As your train comes in, you cannot fail to be impressed by the views of the Tyne and its many bridges. Amongst the locals, chat is invariably about two major topics; how Kevin Keegan's team came so close to winning the title in 1995–96, and the new contemporary art exhibition at the Baltic. There is nothing that the average Geordie loves more than a Mark Wallinger retrospective.

But it is at night that Newcastle becomes the mythical Eighth Wonder of the World. That is when the city centre, or more specifically an area known as the Bigg Market, becomes one of the world's greatest heterosexual meat markets. Impeccably coiffured and groomed men hunt in packs looking for willing participants for a ravaging. Groups of drunk women stumble around on badly chosen heels, hoping that the course of true love will run smooth tonight, while defiantly sending a message to the freezing temperatures that clothes are for losers. DJs play identikit sets of commercial pop interspersed with occasional Bon Jovi.

> ## PRACTICE QUESTION
> How did Newcastle United manage to blow it in 1995–96?

Newcastle on a Saturday night is where to head to if you have not pulled in years. Such are the levels of drunkenness, lust and emotional vulnerability, it is pretty much impossible not to hit some kind of temporary jackpot. If you fail, I'm sorry, but you really need to up your game.

TOP TIPS

VISITING YOUR DOCTOR

Unless you have serious avoidance issues, or are blessed with freakishly good health, you can't get through life without needing the assistance of your local general practitioner. Whether you have serious long-term illnesses, or you just need a chat about last night's episode of *Call the Midwife*, they are there for you. Developing a good relationship with primary care can only be beneficial. So here is the deal.

1   Immunisations are essential for your kids. Forget what you may have read elsewhere.

2   Don't ask for a second opinion. This is the NHS, you have done extremely well to get a first opinion.

3 If the GP asks you to give a urine sample, take at least five minutes. This allows the GP enough time to Google your symptoms.

4 Just once, why not find out how your GP is. It doesn't have to be all about you.

5 Don't ever bring a list.

6 If you don't really speak English, please bring someone who does. A doctor can't diagnose the cause of your chest pain through hand signals alone.

7 Do not dismiss what your GP says just because he is an overweight, problem-drinking chain smoker. He is still an expert, just one with his own self-control issues.

8 If the cream that your GP has prescribed for you has an antifungal, antibacterial and steroidal component, it means that he or she does not have a clue what is wrong with you.

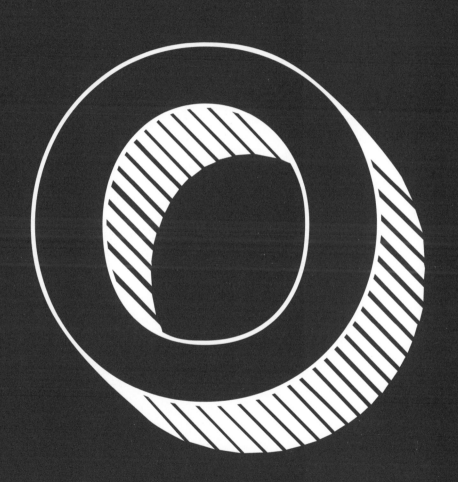

OLYMPIC GAMES

Once upon a time, the city of Paris decided that it really wanted to host an Olympic Games. This idea was too much for the city of London to bear, so it decided, rather spitefully, to put in its own bid. Nobody seriously gave London much of a chance, and as a result nobody was too worried about it. But that was to underestimate the passion and commitment of Sebastian Coe, and the ability of the French to overdo the whole arrogance thing.

In July 2005, the International Olympic Committee made the shock announcement that London would host the 2012 Olympics. The inevitable triumphalist excitement soon gave way to blind panic. Surely, given the city's shoddy transport infrastructure and history of bad government, this Olympics would be a poorly organised disaster?

What actually happened in 2012 will echo in eternity. Or at least it will in London, I am not convinced that the rest of the country necessarily shared the same euphoria. Stadia were completed in time. Trains ran on time. Ordinary citizens spoke to each other with civility and good cheer. People packed pubs to watch cyclists, rowers and dancing horses bring home gold. A Somali-born immigrant called Mohamed twice caused a cheering population to disintegrate into an uncontrolled, quasi-orgasmic mess. By the end of 19 days of incredible competition, Britain had regained its greatness, its pride and its self-confidence. Being patriotic was no longer seen as unseemly, it was now a whole lot of fun. Then came the Paralympics, and the crowd volume was raised to eleven once more.

Everything went *way* over budget, at a cost to the taxpayers, many of whom are still struggling to feel the benefit. It remains to be seen what the nature of the much-heralded 'legacy' is. It may well be up to future sports and economic historians to decide whether London 2012 was as successful as it felt at the time. But it cannot be denied that for a few glorious weeks, London was the best place to be on the planet. And this made France very, very unhappy.

PRACTICE QUESTION

Explain how it came to pass that the ability to teach a horse to dance is seen as an Olympic sport.

ONE DIRECTION

Britain has an extraordinarily rich musical heritage that has been exported all over the globe. I am happy to say that the vast majority of this is down to skill, talent and originality. Then there is the curious case of One Direction.

They didn't even win *The X Factor* (see page 158). None of them look like they could handle themselves in a strong breeze. Not one of them has a voice distinctive enough to carry a solo career, as I suspect Zayn Malik is about to discover. Their music is utterly forgettable, and while they are not bad-looking guys, you wouldn't particularly notice any of them if they walked past you in the street. In terms of actual talent, they make Take That look like the Rolling Stones. And yet their success is both extraordinary in scope, and easy to understand. A lot of pre-teen and teenage girls are very, very stupid, and will slavishly follow just about anything that looks superficially above average. On 1 January 2015, Harry Styles tweeted the word 'Burger'. Two hundred thousand people retweeted it. It is lucky that Louis, Harry, Niall and Liam are essentially nice people, because their potential to start a death cult is considerable.

PRACTICE QUESTION

From memory, hum one of their tunes. Impossible.

ONLY FOOLS AND HORSES

A
B
C
D
E
F
G
H
I
J
K
L
M
N
O
P
Q
R
S
T
U
V
W
X
Y
Z

There are many current TV shows that you need to watch occasionally, just to know what everyone else is talking about. Then there are the shows of the past for which the same is true, because people still talk about them with obsessive reverence.

One such show is *Only Fools and Horses*. It started over 30 years ago with no great fanfare, and yet developed into the one true behemoth of British situation comedy. The plot was simple – a greedy, selfish man behaves in a greedy, selfish, but ultimately forgivable way. Repeat ad infinitum. The characters developed and became strangely loveable, the physical pratfalls were memorable, and the catchphrases have inveigled their way into common English usage.

It is probably not as popular outside of London, but it remains the most likely candidate for Britain's National Sitcom. As such, you need to be very aware of it. Enjoy the falling chandeliers, exploding coaches, unconditional fraternal love and the occasional woman. Overseas, market traders may attempt to grab your attention with the words 'Lovely Jubbly'. It is a compliment – it means they think you are British.

TOP TIP

Do not waste any money on the box set. Simply make sure that your TV deal includes the channel Gold.

The show faded in its final years, but at its best, it was a magnificent monument to just how much Britain loves a roguish underdog.

KATIE PRICE

It should of course go without saying that you want your kids to enjoy the best that British education has to offer, because a good grounding in academia is the best start that your child can have when it comes to maximising their employment potential. Keep drumming this message into your kids, because it won't be long before they discover that there is another way.

Katie Price is worth £45 million. It is an astonishing triumph of ambition and tenacity over discernible talent. Nobody quite knows what she does, apart from willingly put herself under the surgeon's knife. She is certainly a devoted mother, but that does not make her in any way unusual. What makes her unusual is her willingness to bare her soul regarding disastrous relationships and friendships, in a manner that some of the British public simply cannot get enough of. She has 'written' autobiographies, novels and children's books galore, tried to do Eurovision, stood for Parliament, brought out an equestrian fashion range and named one of her daughters Princess Tiaamii Crystal Esther. By any criteria, this is a chaotic life, and one that hardly seems aspirational.

And yet...£45 million. People absolutely love her. Your kids must never find out just how much money can be made from relentless media overexposure.

PRACTICE QUESTION

Outline the conceptual differences between 'Jordan' and 'Katie Price'.

PUBLIC SCHOOLS

I don't know who you are, what job you do, or what you earn. You may see a private education as a necessity for your kids, you may see it as a distant pipe dream.

What cannot be denied is that you need to know this basic truth; the alumni of Britain's public schools run the country. They are Prime Ministers, Chancellors of the Exchequer, London Mayors, Oscar-nominated actors, Mumford & Sons and Frank Lampard. Ever since Old Etonian David Cameron decided to pack his cabinet with fellow public schoolboys, the problem has worsened.

Public schools are remarkable places. The one I went to was in the middle of south-east London, and in the summer, boys in stripy blazers and straw hats would play croquet on the lawn. This sent out a defiant message to the rest of the youth in the area, 'If you want to mug us, we will put up no resistance whatsoever.' I left school with an above average understanding of Latin and a deep antipathy towards Rugby Union. I never thought that my education had prepared me to run the country, but it turns out you simply cannot get anywhere in politics, or indeed acting, unless you went to the right school.

> **PRACTICE QUESTION**
>
> Give five modern practical uses for Latin.

If you are parents, this presents something of a dilemma. Do you cripple yourselves financially just so that your kids can get the chances you didn't have? Your call...

RADIO

The radio is your friend. Local radio stations provide information about events and news in your area, but perhaps more importantly will let you know about traffic black spots and misfiring transport systems. I live in London. I cannot leave the house until my local radio has told me exactly which tiny fraction of the transport system is actually operating.

National radio stations offer more diverse fare.

TalkSPORT deals mostly in football debate with a heady mix of populist right-wing rhetoric. If you are as angry about José Mourinho as you are about gypsies, then this is the station for you.

BBC Radio 1 offers something called 'commercial pop'. If you are anything like me, you will give this a wide berth, decrying the creative bankruptcy of the current music scene, and wondering what happened to proper bands like they had in the 80s.

BBC Radio 2 offers light chat, as well as proper bands like they had in the 80s.

BBC Radio 3 offers classical music. So does the commercial station Classic FM, who play their joker by giving Alan Titchmarsh an opportunity to display his encyclopaedic knowledge of the works of Rachmaninoff. Whether you see the addition as a good or a bad thing is entirely up to you.

BBC Radio 4 offers an entertainment smorgasbord. As long as your tastes are defiantly middle-class. Many of its shows are as old as time itself, barely changing to accommodate for the fact that the world has moved on. It is a world where comedians deemed too old or unattractive for television are allowed to prosper and flourish. Slightly smug wordsmiths play genteel parlour games, politicians and gardeners are forced to answer questions, and women get a whole hour for themselves. Radio 4 is a unique entertainment ecosystem and long may that continue.

BBC Radio 5 Live intersperses news and debate with live sports coverage. It is an interesting mix, and it is not unknown for them to interrupt major news stories with a report on an own goal at Selhurst Park.

BBC Radio 6 Music also has proper bands like they had in the 80s. Only these ones are far more fashionable and far less well-known than those on Radio 2.

I realise that the Internet also provides all this and more. But life in Britain without radio would be very dull indeed.

A
B
C
D
E
F
G
H
I
J
K
L
M
N
O
P
Q
R
S
T
U
V
W
X
Y
Z

SERVICE STATIONS

Motorway driving can be something of an arduous ordeal.
For that reason, hellish watering holes appear at regular
intervals, allowing you to take a breather. This is the perfect
opportunity to fill your tank with petrol at prices way
beyond what you remembered them to be, to eat at Burger
King at prices way beyond what you remembered them to
be, and to buy a 'Best of the 80s' compilation CD, containing
three songs you have heard of and 77 songs that you haven't.

   It is an utterly dispiriting affair, but it is preferable to
falling asleep at the wheel. Just.

TOP TIP

Fill your tank at the start
of your journey, and take
a packed lunch.

WILLIAM SHAKESPEARE

When it comes to playwrights, William Shakespeare is so far ahead of his rivals he can really be seen as Donald Bradman, Roger Federer and Phil 'The Power' Taylor rolled into one. There is simply nobody out there that comes close to the sheer scale of his literary influence.

His plays are not easy reads. Few people say 'forsooth' any more, and the language can certainly seem arcane. But have the patience to stick with it and you cannot fail to be impressed by lavish and sophisticated storytelling on the subjects of love, jealousy, duty, extremes of happiness and despair, power, lust, and baking your enemies in a pie. The death toll is as high as a series of *Game of Thrones*, but with none of the embarrassment of being addicted to a kids' show.

There are several good reasons to make yourself familiar with his work, and cerebral nourishment is undoubtedly one, but perhaps the best one is that British people themselves have not voluntarily read many of his plays. This is your chance to get one over on the British public. If you can quote from one of Hamlet's soliloquies, start a conversation about what exactly happened to Antigonus after he was pursued by a bear, or be able to understand just how violent Scottish kings could be, then nobody could have the cheek to accuse you of not doing enough to 'fit in'. *You* are celebrating Britain's greatest cultural export. Ask *them* what they have done.

Age cannot wither him, nor custom stale his infinite variety. Brush up your Shakespeare.

> ## PRACTICE QUESTION
>
> To be, or not to be?
> That is the question.
> What is the answer?

A
B
C
D
E
F
G
H
I
J
K
L
M
N
O
P
Q
R
S
T
U
V
W
X
Y
Z

THE QUEEN

'Send her victorious, happy and glorious, long to reign over us, God save the Queen.' You are not going to get very far when it comes to fully fledged citizenship if you don't make yourself thoroughly acquainted with those words, and with the woman to whom those words are directed. Britain is a vibrant, modern country, one of the leading economic and cultural nations in the world. And yet, barring occasional republican interludes, power lies in the hands of a single elite family for no other reason than 'well, that is just how things have always been.' Given the enormous potential for the abuse of power, Britain has been a little fortunate with its recent monarchs, who seem a far cry from the assorted despots of centuries past. You will not be expected to know them all. At the end of the day, you are British. What follows is a basic timeline.

1066 William the Conqueror lives up to his nickname.

1189–1199 Richard I spends almost his entire reign picking fights with foreigners. Earns the nickname 'Clarkson'.

1215 A dreadful man called King John seals Magna Carta under a great deal of duress. From now on, by law, monarchs have to have a nice side.

1327 Edward II turns up to Accident and Emergency claiming to have slipped and fallen onto a red-hot poker.

1485 Richard III dies in a Leicester car park, bringing to an end the first of many tedious disputes between Lancashire and Yorkshire.

1558 Mary I dies, along with her habit of burning Protestants alive. Elizabeth I takes over, and despite a long and glorious reign, earns a nickname based on her limited appetite for sexual congress. #everydaysexism

1603 James VI of Scotland becomes James I of England.

1649 Charles I gambles everything. And loses everything, including his head.

1714 The Germans arrive, in the shape of George I. George's inability to speak any English makes the Christmas message a shambles.

1760 George III begins a 60-year reign characterised by madness.

1837 The 64-year reign of Queen Victoria begins. Such is her power, she eventually becomes Empress of India. The Indians were absolutely delighted to be ruled over by a grumpy old widow they had never heard of.

1936 Edward VIII becomes king. Given the choice between royal duty and American totty, he runs off with his girlfriend and becomes mates with Hitler. George VI takes over and begins a heroic battle against a speech impediment.

1952 The King is dead. Long live the Queen.

Few could have predicted that Elizabeth's reign would be quite as long as this, a reign marked by dignified, low-key benevolence. She may be married to a cantankerous old Greek who cannot be trusted within the vicinity of a bottle of port and an African diplomat, her eldest son and heir now wears the permanently hangdog expression of a man who has reluctantly accepted his fate, and, for legal reasons, this book will say nothing on the matter of her other two sons. One of her grandsons is living the dream, combining war, global philanthropy and strip billiards. To her credit, the Queen serenely rises above it all.

It doesn't really matter what you think about the *existence* of the monarchy. It is not about to disappear, as it continues to be hugely popular with an increasingly sycophantic and deferential populace. Yes, this is a bizarre state of affairs, but be thankful that she is not a monster. She is a sweet, elderly lady, who has presided over much personal and national drama, and yet remains unflappable, never once having overextended her reach. Phew.

SHEFFIELD

Like the 'Eternal City' of Rome, Sheffield is traditionally said to have been built on seven hills. That is very much where the similarities end.

Rome has a series of dazzling ancient monuments that draw in tourists in their millions. Sheffield has the Meadowhall Shopping Centre, one of many gigantic temples to British consumerism that can drain your will to live within half an hour.

Sheffield, like Birmingham (see page 30), is far from being visually compelling. But it does have the Crucible Theatre, the spiritual home of a curiously British sport called snooker. Famously, in 1985, 18 million viewers stayed up until well after midnight to watch an Irishman with odd glasses defeat a less interesting ginger-haired man. Nowadays, the most-watched shows on telly are lucky to get 12 million.

Sheffield's chief claim to fame is music. For a relatively unheralded city, it has produced many *great* bands, as well as Def Leppard. Britpop cheerleaders Pulp are the patron saints of the city, while current maestros Arctic Monkeys will certainly make you curious to find out just how grimy the city can get. The answer is 'very'. Thanks to its cultural heritage, Sheffield has far more to it than meets the eye.

TOP TIP

Visit this city when you get a weekend off. Just don't bother to take a camera.

SHERLOCK HOLMES

One of Britain's most-loved fictional characters, Sherlock Holmes appeals to those of us who fantasise about being far cleverer than we actually are. Whether it is genuinely possible to be quite so ultra-intuitive is a debate for another day, because the brilliantly crisp writing of Sir Arthur Conan Doyle convinces us that not only is it possible, but that if Sherlock Holmes was around today, he would reduce ISIS to gibbering wrecks within minutes. Who needs counter-terrorism units when Sherlock could correctly identify a jihadist by examining the way he wears his sandals?

Read the stories for their entertainment value, but also read them to see a portrait of how we would love many of our crime fighters to be. Reliant not on brutal violence, but on being spectacularly good at noticing stuff. How terribly British.

PRACTICE QUESTION

What is the name of his mate, the one we don't really care about?

STONEHENGE

Not even the great Sherlock Holmes has a clue how these stones got to Salisbury Plain. Nobody does. It is one of the great joys of living in Britain to drive down an extremely nondescript section of the A303 and then suddenly come across the most famous Neolithic monument in the world.

Those stones are enormous. For all the decades of analysis about what the exact pattern actually signifies, it may just be that approximately 4,600 years ago, a group of people were carrying these massive rocks and just gave up through sheer exhaustion. We will never know the truth. So you might as well make up your own theories, and simply enjoy its weird, ethereal beauty.

PRACTICE QUESTION

If it takes one man 17 months to move a one-ton rock a distance of 50 miles, how long will it take 400 men to move 93 one-ton rocks a distance of 200 miles?

STRICTLY COME DANCING

This show is an all-powerful juggernaut that displays no sign of slowing down. The concept is simple. A selection of soap stars, retired sports stars and those celebrities from the 70s and 80s who have not been touched by Operation Yewtree get together with a professional partner and learn how to dance.

Some of them are utterly, grotesquely awful. But the audience wishes them well, as they know what it's like to have to pay a tax bill. Others are pretty good from the start and improve week on week. Eventually the winner is announced, and nobody mentions the victor's childhood dance lessons at stage school. Repeat again next year.

TOP TIP

Do not try any of these moves at home.

As with so much successful television, the scale of its popularity is hard to fathom. The dancing is rarely good enough or bad enough to be interesting, and the musical arrangements can be appalling. Feel your soul disintegrate as you see 'Anarchy in the UK' turned into a bossa nova.

Perhaps, though, the show's massive appeal is simply that it is safe, comforting fun that the whole family can enjoy. And this is increasingly rare.

A
B
C
D
E
F
G
H
I
J
K
L
M
N
O
P
Q
R
S
T
U
V
W
X
Y
Z

SUPERMARKETS

They are everywhere. And they cater for every budget. Within ten years the humble independent food shop may become a thing of the past as the march of the supermarkets continues its relentless path.

At one end of the economic spectrum, Aldi and Lidl offer all the brand names you have never heard of at amazing prices. Pedigree Chunk? Tollgate toothpaste? Tom and Jerry's Ice Cream?

At the other end of the spectrum, Waitrose and Marks & Spencer offer solace to middle-class families for whom happiness is a particular brand of Kalamata olives that will drive their friends green with envy.

In between these extremes are the supermarket behemoths: Morrisons, Sainsbury's, Asda and pantomime villain Tesco. This is where you will spend much of your adult life. Indeed, if you can afford to get your food delivered to your home, you don't really need this book at all.

The big four supermarkets are in fierce competition and will try all kinds of tricks to lure you in, including surprise discounts, longer opening hours or treating the customer with courtesy. Go with your own bags, or you will be made to feel like you are destroying the planet. And learn how to master the self-checkout machines. This is the key to supermarket happiness. Master these machines and you never have to look into the cold dead eyes of the till assistant again.

TOP TIP

Pointing out that it should read 'Eight items or *fewer*' may give you satisfaction, but wins you no friends among supermarket staff.

MARGARET THATCHER

You can't call yourself British unless you have an opinion on the most divisive British politician of all time. It doesn't really matter what your opinion is, as long as it is passionately held.

To some, she was the saviour of the modern British state. She took over a country left in ruins by militant trade unions and the infamous 'Winter of Discontent', and grabbed the nation by its metaphorical balls. Thanks to a programme of industrial reorganisation, and allowing people to dare to dream about social mobility, she taught Britain how to be great again. What's more, when the Argentines made their misguided attempt to grab a patch of the South Atlantic that will be forever British, she did not flinch in showing them who was boss.

To others she was Satan's spawn, a despotic mix of tyranny and evil, who took a scythe to working-class pride and tried hard to replace it with the slavish worship of corporate greed. Her premiership was a reign of terror, her rivals cowed, the electorate bullied into voting for her again and again.

That is the dichotomy with Thatcher. Some people did brilliantly out of her. Some people did catastrophically badly. Your perspective on her legacy rather depends on whether you are a Falkland Islander, a city broker or a former South Yorkshire coal miner. But you have to have an opinion. And it helps the flow of conversation if it is an extreme one.

TOP TIP

If you are a passionate Thatcher fan, think carefully about where you choose to express your opinions.

TOWIE

TOWIE stands for *The Only Way is Essex*. It is a controversial statement of intent, and one wonders just how hellish the question might be for which that could possibly constitute a valid answer.

When the show first started, a lot of people were aghast at just how moronic television had become. The show is a look at the lives of superficially attractive young people. Unfortunately, these are profoundly unintelligent people lacking any social graces, and their lives are about as interesting as an unsolicited PPI phone call. And yet the programme is a massive success. Abetted by a tabloid press that is only too happy to fill its newspapers with photographs of cast members stumbling out of limousines and into nightclubs that you wouldn't be seen dead in, somehow the show has become part of the cultural fabric of the nation.

Gasp in amazement as someone you don't care about files her nails. Laugh heartily as the token gay guy shrieks hysterically and says something about S Club 7. Enjoy laddish 'banter'. Repeat ad infinitum. Your kids will love this show. Please try to wean them off it, and encourage them to pursue their educational dreams. Unlike the 'stars' of *Made in Chelsea* (see page 106), these are not bad people. They are just dim people, and should not be used as role models under any circumstances.

TOP TIP

There are lots of other television channels.

THE GREAT BRITISH PUB

1 Don't order a half-pint unless you are extremely secure in your sexuality.

2 It is two shots on the black. It has always been two shots on the black, and the rules are clearly displayed on the wall. Point this out to your opponent before you start your game. He will appreciate your candour and respect you forever.

3 Don't be fooled. The quiz machine is never about to pay out. Just when you think it is, that is when the question about Everton's annual attendance during the 1927–28 season rears its unwelcome head.

4 Every so often, people will enter the pub for no other reason than to sell you cheap DVDs. Buy them. What is the worst that can happen? You have just watched *Dallas Buyers Club* for a quid, and helped to feed a family of four in Shanghai.

5 You won't win the pub quiz unless you have a smartphone that is both easy to use and easy to hide.

6 No matter how many people are in the pub, the average time between your jukebox selection and you hearing your song is somewhere in the region of three hours.

7 Unless one of you has any kind of track record of hitting a double successfully, don't even start a game of darts. The sight of two grown men throwing at double one for 20 minutes demeans everyone.

8 If your local is a real-ale pub, you will fit in much better if you don't shave for two months and put on three stone.

9 Even if a venue labels itself as a gastropub, don't expect too much on the culinary front. The good news is that pork scratchings and Scampi Fries effectively bridge the gap between crisps and actual food.

10 If it has been decided that it's your round, then it is definitely your round. It doesn't matter that you have never met the person who has decided that it is your round. Do the honourable thing. The alternative – never being welcome in your own local pub again – is too horrible to contemplate.

BATTLE OF TRAFALGAR

Much of the British public are clueless about history, so it is good to name-drop some historical events into conversation to validate your Britishness. For this purpose, the Battle of Trafalgar is perfect because it is undoubtedly, beautifully, heroically British.

The reason for this is the tragic fate of the hero of the piece. A one-eyed, one-armed admiral with a legendary reputation for skills in naval battle, Lord Nelson began 21 October 1805 by stating that 'England expects that every man will do his duty', and ended it lifeless, below decks, having just asked his best mate Hardy for a quick kiss.

During the day, Nelson had been overseeing that most traditional of British achievements, that is, defeating the French. As with Agincourt that preceded it, and Waterloo that soon followed, it is important to have a working understanding of those skirmishes in which we vanquished our loathed rivals.

> **TOP TIP**
>
> 'Kiss me Hardy' – it meant nothing. Do not try to claim otherwise.

UNIVERSITY

You may have come to the UK to study. Or you may have come here to work so that one day your kids can study. Either way, a university education is a mighty fine thing. It also comes at a very heavy price.

Britain cannot move for universities. The two most famous ones, Oxford and Cambridge, have colleges that will astonish you with their serene beauty, a beauty that seems wasted on the booze-addled young. Fey men and earnest women cycle around these two cities, safe in the knowledge that there is every chance that their three years of studious hard work will set them up for life, especially if they are planning a career in media or politics.

Unless your kids are geniuses, though, Oxbridge may well be a fantasy. There are dozens of other great universities, such as Manchester, Edinburgh and Leeds. If you want all the social elitism of Oxbridge with a fraction of the guaranteed employment success, you can try Durham. More controversially, there are 'lesser' universities, which look like amazing places to spend three years, but which dish out degrees of more debatable value. This is where the dilemmas arise.

Because a university degree is expensive, up to £9,000 per year. To graduate in medicine may seem like a justifiable return on the investment. To leave with a degree in media studies from London Metropolitan University seems like a recipe for financial ruin.

Further education is a noble and life-enriching endeavour. But you want a degree? Well, a degree costs. And right here is where you start paying.

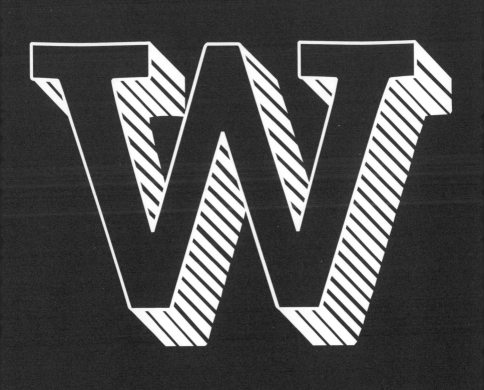

WALES

Wales is just beautiful. I speak as a man who has fond childhood memories of holidays in The Mumbles, the locals being deceived by my parents' accents into thinking they were from Abergavenny.

The entrance fee is steep, but the Severn Bridge, with its stunning views, acts as a gateway to a magical land of all-male choirs, mountains and valleys and declining former mining towns, all redolent with the aroma of 1970s Rugby Union. Living and working there is quite a good idea – not least because you can get a six-bedroom detached house in Ebbw Vale for the price of a studio flat in London. Furthermore, taking a holiday there is an alluring alternative to foreign travel. Do not just visit Cardiff (page 42); there are beautiful stretches of coastline, magnificent castles and opportunities to hike, climb, kayak and other stuff I have never actually done.

What's more, the Welsh don't seem quite as angry as the Scots.

TOP TIP

Learn by heart the commentary to Gareth Edwards' try against the All Blacks in 1973. You will be a hero.

THE X FACTOR

So now we come to the last of the so-called 'water-cooler' television shows in this book. In theory, *The X Factor* comes from a long line of talent shows that goes back many decades. However, there are aspects to this show that differ slightly from those of its forebears.

Firstly, none of the judges in the show have ever had what could be described as 'music credibility'. In particular, nobody quite knows what Louis Walsh's contribution to the music industry actually consists of.

Secondly, it was decided some time ago that many of the worst contestants were so bad, it would make great telly to exploit their mental fragility and have them mocked in front of the nation.

Thirdly, at least one of the bad contestants will make it to the televised stage, just so that people will watch and be enraged. And then watch again next week.

And fourthly, and most importantly, it doesn't matter who wins, as 2007 winner Leon Jackson can confirm. The winner is whoever Simon Cowell takes the biggest liking to (see page 124).

It is all formulaic nonsense, and perhaps its declining viewing figures are partly because people can see through its cynicism. It is still one of the biggest shows on the box, through, and the main reason you need to know about its workings and its stars is that your kids will obsess over it.

PRACTICE QUESTION

What is Leon Jackson doing now?